HEAVEN'S PEAK

MIGUEL ESTRADA

Table of Contents

THE HUNT

CHAPTER 1

The crunchy sound of the leaves beneath his feet was satisfying. With each step, Rudy Everett jumped to avoid the puddles that had filled the forest the night before. The trees sobbed around him, thick drops falling on his head.

He liked to pretend he was an explorer, living countless adventures that would put most of his favorite movie characters to shame.

A solemn breeze made its way through the trees, which had already begun to take on the warm colors of autumn. The accompanying sound was a spectral whisper that made Rudy imagine all sorts of situations: a giant hiding in the earth's depths, who had been awakened from his long sleep, or perhaps the voices of the forest's spirits, whispering.

He reached into his pocket to pull out his walkie-talkie. His dad had bought the set for his birthday. Rudy shared the other one with his best friend and neighbor, Junior. Since he lived next door, they didn't have any problems using it unless the batteries ran out. Grinning from ear to ear, Rudy pressed the power button.

He deepened his voice as much as he could and referred to himself as private detective Rudy Everett, on the trail of a criminal nearby. The only response was white noise, which meant he was too far away to talk to Junior.

The cold air reddened his cheeks; he tried to contain a sneeze but failed. Rudy wiped his nose with his sweater's sleeve and looked up. Orange beams of sunlight peeked through the branches.

It was getting late. He'd better go home before his mom got too worried. If his mom got worried, his dad would get upset; if his dad got upset, his sisters would get mad; and when his sisters got mad, it was bad news. It wasn't worth the drama just because little Rudy had decided to play outside a little longer than usual. It was unfair, he wasn't a baby anymore. In a few months, he would be eight years old, more than enough to decide how much time to spend outside. He laughed at the thought of saying that to his mom. She would never listen, but it was nice to have dreams.

Rudy turned, walking faithfully across the dirt road from which he had come. Even though the trip was already familiar, he always found new things to be excited about. A tree he hadn't noticed was leaning to one side, a colorful flower that wasn't there last summer, some scratches carved into the trunk of an oak tree...

He stopped dead in his tracks. Those scratches weren't there before. Not last summer, not last week, not even when he passed by an hour ago. Rudy looked around, trembling, waiting for a huge dark-haired bear to jump out from behind the bushes. It wasn't possible; his dad had told him there were no bears in that area. If there were any, his family would never have allowed him to play outside in the first place. That thought reassured him a little. He took a deep breath before continuing on.

His walk turned into a trot and he cast furtive glances over his shoulder, alert to any movement, any noise out of the ordinary. A tree appeared out of nowhere, Rudy had to raise his hands to avoid bumping into it. He stopped and looked up at the oak, which was becoming a shadow in the approaching night.

Rudy rubbed his head, confused. There shouldn't have been anything in his way. It took a moment for him to realize he was no longer walking on the dirt road, which meant he had deviated from the path at some point. He looked down. His feet were covered in a dense blanket of darkness. His heart raced, his lungs asking desperately for more air. He had to get out of there, fast. He raised his hands, grasping the branches around him to guide his way. His teeth chattered as his nose exhaled white smoke. He couldn't afford to spend the night in the middle of the woods, especially with wild animals lurking in the shadows and watching him with hungry eyes. Rudy quickened his pace.

Among the trees in the distance, he could see a tall figure whose body seemed to blend in with the surroundings. Daylight was almost gone, so he had to squint to distinguish the figure from the foliage. It looked like a person.

Rudy bolted toward it. Dodging rocks and skipping over puddles, the little boy made his way to the mysterious man.

As he approached, he realized the man was taller than he'd thought, bigger than any adult Rudy had ever known in his short life. The man's arms stretched grotesquely to his knees and his body was covered by a long black coat. His face hidden behind a black-eyed mask that seemed to be embedded in his skin, no, rather, it was as if the mask was part of his skin. A chill ran down the back of Rudy's neck. He swallowed, gathered all the courage he could, and whispered, out of breath:

"H-hello... uh... I'm Rudy, I'm a bit lost, and I need help getting home..."

The man in black just stared at him.

"Why are you wearing that mask? It's not Halloween yet." Rudy tried to force a smile. "I also like to put on costumes. I live nearby, and I think there's a bear or something, and it's already getting dark, so can you take me to my house?"

The man remained silent. There was something in that mask's empty gaze that disturbed Rudy greatly. His heart throbbed in his throat, but he had to swallow his fear. If there was anything dangerous in the woods, that man could help him get back to his family safely.

The masked man stepped forward, breaking a branch on the ground with his heavy boots as he approached. Without realizing it, Rudy found himself taking a step back as the man leaned closer to him.

A strange noise came from the boy's jacket. With a jolt, he realized that it was his walkie-talkie crackling with white noise. He looked down for a fraction of a second and, when he looked up again, the mask was only a few inches away from his face. Rudy screamed with all the strength of his lungs and darted away.

With no sense of direction and in total darkness, he sprinted as far as he could, pushing branches out of his way. He could almost feel the man's breath on his neck as he plunged deeper into the forest.

Rudy stumbled and fell on his face against the damp earth. He tried to get back up between sobs, with scratches on his arms and knees, covered in mud. Before he could stand, a pair of black boots appeared in front of him. He tried to resist the temptation to look up but failed. His gaze met those eyes, dark like night itself.

That creepy image was the last thing the boy saw. After that, complete darkness.

CHAPTER 2

The golden sunrays spread over the now reddish mountains. Below, a concrete road wound around the hills. The only car passing by was a red Mustang. The driver, John Miller, sighed in awe. It had been seventeen years since the last time he saw the sunset decorating that beautiful landscape, like an artistic painting waiting to be created. He'd never been the artist type, but his children were both prodigies, to him at least.

He adjusted the rearview mirror to take a better look at his eight-year-old daughter, Jenny. The little girl slept with her head pressed against the window, and a thread of saliva fell on the stuffed dog she held tightly. In the passenger seat was Kevin, his teenage son, inspecting the camera he had just bought with his own hard-earned money. The boy had spent almost the entire summer saving. After all, it was one of those new fancy models, and technology of such caliber didn't come cheap.

John smiled, filled with immense pride.

"Is it good?" he asked.

"One of the best," said Kevin, staring at the camera.

"For its price, it better be," said John. He waited for a reply, but Kevin just stared out the window. Strike one. John tried again. "It's beautiful, don't you think? Why don't you take a picture?"

"Uhh, no. Maybe if I had a better angle."

Strike two.

"Heaven's Peak is such a beautiful town, you know, I think both of you are going to love it. Nature, the people, everything is so peaceful and gorgeous. Besides, I'm sure it's not going to be hard for you to make new friends. Change is always difficult, but it's necessary to grow, you know, as people." Kevin sat back as if he hadn't heard him. John took a deep breath. "You know, this is where your mom and I first met. I had come on a vacation with my family, and she was on some sort of student's exchange program. God... she was so beautiful." John couldn't stop his eyes from watering. "Then we came for our honeymoon and stayed in a hotel with a view of the mountains. That is why I decided that if we are going to start a new life, let it be here."

"I know, Dad. You've told us that story a million times," Kevin said. He leaned over, turned on the radio, and adjusted the volume. John pondered for a couple of minutes, trying to come up with a topic of interest that would coax some words out of his son, but having a conversation with him was like trying to pull out a tooth.

It hadn't always been like that. The death of his wife was a heavy blow to him and the children. At the time, the concept of death was something foreign for Jenny. John had tried to explain to her that her mom was asleep and would not wake up, but Jenny insisted she would. In the end, it was Kevin who had a conversation with her that made her understand the situation.

Kevin glanced at his sister in the backseat, like a dog guarding its pup.

Between the announcer talking nonsense on the radio and his daughter sleeping, John decided to throw in the towel. If he were lucky, a change of atmosphere would be enough to cut the distance between them. Kevin handled his camera carefully as if afraid that it would break, and took a picture of the mountains.

John smiled. A bright future awaited them in Heaven's Peak.

CHAPTER 3

The picture of a smiling child slid across the desk, his golden hair falling over bright eyes full of joy. FBI agent Norman James ran his hand over his chin, trying to hide his frustration. At that moment, the poor boy could be in danger or, perhaps by then, already six feet underground.

"Rudy Everett," said Sheriff Gordon, leaning back in a desk chair that struggled to contain his considerable weight. "Seven years old, last seen by one of his sisters, who claims that he went to play in the clearing behind their house. It's something he would do all the time, except this time he didn't come back for dinner. I have officers investigating the area but with no success. It's like the kid vanished in thin air, just like the others. Two months ago, it was the Madisons' daughter. Good family; I've known them for years. Decent people. A few months before that, a boy decided his mother was taking too long to pick him up at school, so he decided to walk home and went missing also. He lived two blocks from his school, can you believe that? Two blocks away and he disappeared. Nobody saw anything, and nobody said anything. Unbelievable."

"How many people have disappeared in the last five years, Sheriff?" Norman asked, sliding the photo back. He didn't want to look at it any longer.

"With the Everett's kid, twenty-seven."

"And there's no common thread between them, nothing at all," said Norman, raising an eyebrow.

"I know how it sounds, Agent, but there doesn't seem to be anything connecting the victims. Most of the recent ones have been children, but before that, they had nothing in common. Men, women, children, adults, tall ones and short ones. This crazy son of a bitch doesn't discriminate against anyone. He seems to choose his victims at random."

Agent James rested his elbow on the arm of the chair. "Do you seriously believe a single person is responsible for all of that?"

"We can't discard anything yet," said Gordon with a defiant look. The man was in his early sixties but the only things that seemed to prove it were his snowy white hair and his eyes, which carried the weight of a person who has lived through many things. "With the little evidence we have, we can't be sure."

"Except it doesn't make any sense."

"If you have something to say, Agent, enlighten me."

"A single person can't have done all of that. It doesn't make any sense. Serial killers usually have a specific type of victim, like women of

10

their own ethnic group or something like that. All of these victims have been different, only recently they've been children. There's no reason to assume that the same person is responsible for all of these kidnappings. Besides, at some point he would've made a mistake, someone would have seen something, or he would have left something behind."

"So what's your hypothesis?"

James adjusted his tie. He was used to presenting his ideas to his superiors in the FBI, but there was something about Gordon, the sheriff of a small town in the middle of nowhere, that intimidated him. Perhaps it was his presence, which reminded him of his late father.

"I think it's an organized group. They might be involved in human trafficking, which would explain why not a single body has been found. The victims could be taken to other countries and sold on the black market as sex slaves or labor. It wouldn't be the first time. I've seen stuff like that happen before. However, the lack of evidence is surprising. It shows a very sophisticated level of planning. The reason why the victims are so varied could be because they qualify in parameters that we don't know..."

"A fascinating theory," Gordon said sarcastically.

"But even so, how is it possible that something like this continues for so long under the police's nose? I don't think your officers are that incompetent."

"So, what are you implying, Agent?" The sheriff's face turned stern.

"Nothing that hasn't gone through your mind at least once. The people responsible, or at least one of them, must be familiar with police procedures. It's the only explanation I see for how this has been going for so long. They might be working side-by-side with the police, or they may even be some of your own people."

The sheriff raised his eyebrows. He reached into his desk, took out a cigar, pulled out a lighter from his pocket and lit it, inhaling as deeply as he could. As he exhaled, the smoke went directly into James' face.

Gordon stared straight into the agent's eyes.

"Of course it has crossed my mind. There's no night when I don't consider the possibility that one of my men is capable of such an atrocity. The only thing that lets me sleep at night is the certainty that, sooner or later, we'll catch him." The smell of tobacco flooded the entire office. "But lately the kidnappings have been more frequent. People are getting more scared and less willing to help with the investigation. When it began, everyone had something to say. Now nobody talks. They've lost hope. That is why my superiors forced me to bring in help from the FBI. That's the sole reason why you're here, Agent. If it were up to me, you would not be sitting in that chair right now."

James swallowed, buttoned his flawless suit as he stood up and held out his hand to the sheriff. With a wry smile, he said, "It will be a pleasure to work with you."

Gordon took a puff of his cigar and shook the agent's hand without breaking eye contact.

"Officially, you are involved in the investigation, but I recommend that you stay on the sidelines. Don't interfere with our work and everything will go nicely, understood?"

"I won't make any promises, Sheriff." James' grip was as firm as cement. "I understand I'll use a private office, won't I?"

"Yes, at the end of the hallway," Gordon replied. "I cannot wait to see your talent in action."

Those words echoed with a familiar tone of sarcasm. James turned and walked to the door.

"Oh, before I forget," said Gordon. James stopped short as he reached the knob. "Let me introduce the lieutenant in charge of the case."

The sheriff staggered his way to the door and popped out his head into the hallway, looking both sides before beckoning to someone. A few seconds later, a bearded man in his forties approached.

"Thank you, Chief," the bearded man said in a raspy voice. He held out his hand to James and shook it firmly. "Name's Cleyton. Lieutenant Spencer Cleyton. It's a pleasure to finally meet you."

That sarcastic tone again.

"Likewise, Lieutenant. I'm Agent Norman James of the FBI."

"I know, oh, believe me, I know. Everybody at the station has gone crazy over the FBI coming in. I figured it was a matter of time."

"Then let's begin."

Cleyton led him to a door at the end of the corridor. Every office had plates with the respective names and positions of their occupants. The one the lieutenant pointed out, however, had none. The wood of the door was corroded by time and the frame covered by a thick layer of dust. It looked like the janitor's room.

James wrinkled his nose, put his hand on the knob, and took a glance at his future companion, who was grinning from ear to ear. He pushed open the door, which answered with a metallic screech. A desk and a pair of archive shelves occupied half of the room. The space was so small that James had to maneuver to reach the other side of the desk without knocking down the mountain of papers and folders that lay on top of it.

"Well, it looks like you have a lot of homework to do," Cleyton said.

The lieutenant closed the door behind him. James leaned back in his new chair with caution, as he was sure it would fall apart at any moment. With a sigh, he began to read through the first stack of papers within his grasp. He didn't care if he wasn't welcome at the station, he had a job to do, and he was ready to do it, with or without help. James remembered the boy's picture. If he was right, then the kid may still be alive; he might even still be in the town. There was no time to lose. He had a long night to catch up.

CHAPTER 4

⁓

It was a child, or at least the shadow of a child, running through the woods. The leaves were pale blue, gradually decaying to gray. The kid's shadow moved fast, mingling with the vegetation around him as he trod through puddles red as blood.

A man lurked in the dark, waiting for the boy to run into him. The man's height seemed to rival that of the trees around him. He wore coal-black clothing, and his face was white with dark spots where his eyes must have been. A mask seemed to be clinging to his skin.

The boy stumbled and fell into one of the blood-red puddles. Drenched, he tried to sit up, but the masked figure was already standing in front of him. A heartbreaking cry echoed in the night.

Sofia Everett woke up. Her long golden hair stuck to her forehead and shoulders. Her hands trembled uncontrollably, her whole body bathed in icy sweat, glued to the sheets. She took several shallow breaths as her vision adjusted to the darkness.

The tree branches outside her window creaked with the breeze. Under the moonlight and the lampposts, the shadows gave a spectral tour through her bedroom. It was the fifth, or maybe sixth time that had happened. The images lasted only fractions of a second, but they were more vivid than life itself, and they repeated, over and over again, only for her to wake up and realize that it was just a nightmare. Except that it wasn't just a nightmare. She knew who that lost child was—her brother, Rudy.

Sofia felt as if a knife pierced her chest as she remembered him, smiling as he always did, playing without worry. She tried to hold back the tears but couldn't. She pulled her knees to her chest, sitting on the bed and sobbing until she had no more tears left.

The door of the room was ajar, the light from the hallway leaked in and forced her out of her trance. Her sister Lia peered into the room slowly, her green eyes narrowed.

"I'm fine," lied Sofia.

"You don't sound fine."

Lia entered the room, closed the door cautiously behind her and blindly approached Sofia. Groping the mattress in front of her, she sat down on the edge of the bed. Lia took a long breath and finally asked:

"You dreamed about him again, didn't you?"

Sofia nodded. It took her a second to realize that Lia still couldn't see her well, so she made an effort to respond.

"Yes."

"It wasn't your fault."

"Stop saying that. You know it was."

Lia lowered her head. Lia was fifteen, only a year younger than Sofia and they looked pretty much alike, but Sofia always considered Lia to be prettier. She was thinner, her hair lighter and livelier. Sofia's eyes were brown while her sister's seemed to glow in the dark.

"You remind me of him," Sofia confessed.

"Why?"

"He looked just like you." Sofia made an effort to hold back the tears. "I am the black sheep."

"You got Dad's genes," said Lia with a wink. Sofia could not help but smile. "What makes you say that?"

"I don't know. I just think you'd be better off without me."

"Don't be stupid," Lia replied, placing her hand on her sister's shoulder.

"Rudy needed me, and I wasn't there."

"It could've happened to any of us," said Lia, though she didn't sound convinced of her own words.

"Of course not, neither Mom nor Dad would've let him out, and you would have had his eyes on him all the time."

"Maybe, or maybe not. What matters is not what could have been, but what it is now."

"You know they won't find him."

"Don't say that!" Lia shouted.

The door handle turned, the light outside flooded the room, and their father's silhouette appeared in the doorway. Sofia hid her face between her knees.

"Is everything okay, girls?"

"Everything's good, Daddy," Lia replied, settling herself in front of Sofia to cover her. "I just had to ask Sofia about an assignment for this week."

"At two o'clock in the morning?"

"If I leave it for later, I'll forget."

"Okay," he said after a pause. "But don't take too long, it's school night."

"We know, Daddy, don't worry."

"All right."

Sofia waited to hear her father's footsteps fade as far as possible before looking up again. As she did so, she found her sister's melancholic eyes fixed on hers.

"Thank you," said Sofia.

"Don't mention it."

"He's going to keep acting like this, isn't he? As if nothing happened."

"I think it's his way of dealing with everything." Lia's attention moved to the window with a thoughtful look on her face.

"He hardly talks now."

"I can't stand to sit at the table with them anymore. Everything's so quiet."

Sofia pulled her knees even closer to her chest.

"W-we have to do something, Lia."

"What can we do? Let the police do their job."

"We could go to the woods, where Rudy went."

"You're losing your mind," Lia said, kissing her younger sister on the forehead. "Stop thinking those things. You're the only one that I can count on now."

Lia left the room. Outside, the night's wind whistled. Sofia slumped onto the soft mattress. She couldn't just let go of something like that. She had heard the stories, people vanishing without a trace, leaving behind broken hearts and families. She could not let that happen to her family. And Rudy, the poor boy was probably scared to death. It had been years since the first disappearance was in the news. The whole town was shocked at the time, but now it seemed mundane. Who could do something so horrendous? And how was it that, after all this time, not only the person responsible hadn't been caught, but he was adding more victims to the list?

Sofia closed her eyes, fully aware she would not be able to sleep for the rest of the night.

CHAPTER 5

Kevin slowed his pace until he reached the woman in glasses looking out for the children in the park. He'd been running like a horse, but now he could finally breathe with relief as his heart rate slowed. He shook his shirt against his chest to dry the sweat. It was one of those last hot days of fall, and the trees surrounding the park had already turned to the colors of fire.

"I'm sorry, teach, I came as fast as I could," Kevin panted. "My dad was supposed to come for her, but... I don't know. Who knows what's on his mind. He should've gotten out of work by now."

"Don't worry, Kevin," Miss Ashworth replied with a smile. "I'm just glad you were home when I called. Jenny has been here for a while, and she must be getting bored. I don't mind looking after her though. She is such a delight."

The teacher returned her attention to the children. The park was small but had a variety of places to play. Jenny was on the swings, hurtling back and forth so fast she could fly off at any moment. If it were any other girl, Kevin would have stopped her to tell her that it was dangerous to swing so high, but not Jenny. He trusted her. Besides, she was very smart for her age, so any lecture he would come up with would surely have crossed the girl's mind already.

"She's a sunshine," said Kevin. "Thanks."

"Any time," she replied, showing off a perfect white smile.

"How's she doing in class? Does she get along with the other kids?"

"In class, wonderful. Her writing is impeccable; she answers all the questions I ask. She is a bright and talented young girl, and the drawings she makes in her spare time are beautiful. I'm just afraid she's a bit too shy."

"She still doesn't talk to the other kids, does she?"

"Not much, and it's been two weeks since she started here."

"It may take some time to adjust, but she will."

Miss Ashworth nodded. "I understand that it's a new place, an environment perhaps very different from the one she was used to before, but she has to be a little more outgoing. Interact more with her peers, you know?"

"Yes, of course." Kevin sighed. "It's just that, you know, it's all been tough for us."

"I imagine. Jenny sure misses her friends from her former school."

"I doubt that's the reason."

She raised an eyebrow, intrigued. "What do you think it is, then?"

"Our mom." Kevin tried to keep his voice from breaking. "She passed away about six months ago."

"Oh, my God," she said, covering her mouth with her hand. "How awful. I'm so sorry, Kevin. I didn't know."

"Yeah, no, that's okay."

"It must've been so hard, losing her mom at such a young age. Children are more susceptible to a loss, you know? I'm so sorry. Please don't hesitate to call me if you need some advice or help with anything, okay?"

"Thanks."

The two gazed silently at little Jenny, who stepped off from the swings to climb on the slide. She hadn't yet noticed her brother's presence, so it would be the perfect opportunity to take a picture.

Kevin slid his bag over his shoulder, opened it, and pulled out his camera. The warm colors of the trees contrasted with the dry leaves on the ground; some oaks were already naked. He tried to frame the image as best he could to capture everything around his sister, putting Jenny going down the slide right in the middle, surrounded by beautiful orange hues. The girl let go and let gravity do its job as she raised her hands in the air. Kevin took the photo; the flash was barely visible in daylight, but Jenny saw it. With a huge smile, she ran to her brother the moment her feet touched the ground. She threw himself at Kevin with open arms like the wings of a bird about to fly. He managed to catch her, barely keeping his balance and holding onto the camera.

"Booger! You've been good, haven't you? Your teacher tells me you've been farting in class. Is that true?"

"What? No, I didn't!" Jenny shrieked.

The teacher chuckled.

"How could she have lied to me like that?" Kevin said with mock indignation.

He lowered his sister to the floor and ruffled her hair.

"Don't do that, I'm not a boy," Jenny protested, smoothing her mussed locks.

"My work here is done," said Miss Ashworth.

"Thank you again, teach," Kevin said.

"As I told you, it's a pleasure for me to take care of Jenny. You should talk to your dad to make a schedule of what days he can come for her."

"I will."

"Thank you, Miss Ashworth," said Jenny.

"You're welcome, princess. I'll see you tomorrow in class."

The teacher turned and headed home.

"Miss? She's not married, then," said Kevin after watching her disappear.

"She's too old for you," Jenny said with a stern look.

"I just asked if she was married," Kevin said. "Besides, whenever I say something about a girl, you complain about her."

"I'm the only girl in your life," Jenny said with a smile. "You cannot have a girlfriend because you have to take care of me."

"So I'll be single my whole life?"

"No, only until I get married."

Kevin laughed. She looked at him with disdain.

"Don't get mad," he said. He knelt, put his hands in her armpits, and carried her over his shoulders. He liked to pretend that he was stronger than he actually was, and his arms ached every time he did it. Jenny had become much heavier in the last couple of years, so much that he could barely hold her for a few seconds, but he didn't want to spoil her the image of him as the strong older brother, not yet.

"Take another picture," said Jenny.

He lowered her gently to the ground, and his muscles relaxed. "Okay, booger, let me see where the best spot would be."

He glanced around the almost abandoned park. For some reason, the few children who were playing had already left with their parents. It was still early, so there was no reason for the place to be so empty, especially when a few minutes ago it was overflowing with activity.

Cold air caressed his skin. The swings rocked back and forth even though the breeze wasn't even strong enough to even move the leaves on the ground. He swallowed and suddenly had the urge to run to his house without looking back.

"What do you say if I take your picture at the house?" Kevin asked, forcing a smile.

"I already have a bunch of pictures of me at home," Jenny protested, stomping her foot.

"I'll take it on the way back then."

"Please," Jenny begged with large, puppy eyes.

Kevin paused. "Only one."

Jenny jumped in excitement. Kevin put his hands on the camera, it felt heavier somehow, weighting his neck down. With his fingers on the cold metal, he pointed the camera in his sister's direction. She sat on a swing and smiled. He pressed the button, paying no attention to the image's composition, the lighting, or anything else. He just wanted to get rid of that eerie feeling that was eating him up from the inside; he was convinced that someone was watching. His eyes, however, told him that they were the only ones there.

He lowered the camera to his chest and narrowed his eyes to see the trees shivering behind his sister.

"How do I look? Do I look pretty?" Jenny asked with excitement.

The little girl's voice was a distant echo. All of Kevin's attention was focused on the dense woods surrounding the park. He raised his camera again and pressed the button, the lens watching the shadows between the oaks. If he couldn't trust his own senses, maybe his camera could make a difference.

"Kev!"

Her sister's voice made him jump. "Son of a—"

"Don't swear."

"You scared me." Kevin took one last look around, grabbed Jenny's hand and nodded. "Let's get out of here. It's getting late."

By the time she opened her mouth to protest, they were already crossing the street. Kevin looked over his shoulder occasionally to make sure no one was following them.

As they walked away from the park, his pulse returned to normal; little by little he regained his composure. He assumed he'd just had a panic attack, but he'd never felt anything like it, not even when he'd heard that his mother had died alone in a cold hospital bed.

The sun behind the mountains had painted the sky orange by the time they reached their house. Inside, it looked dark as night. All the blinds were shut, and the lights were off. Once Kevin closed the door behind him, they were shrouded in the gloom. He felt his sister's hand tighten around his. The other hand groped the wall looking for the light switch. He found it and flipped it.

For a split second, the flash of the lamp blinded them. He had to blink several times before opening his eyes completely. It wasn't surprising in the slightest to see his father passed out on the couch.

Kevin put one knee on the floor, crouching to Jenny's height and doing his best to smile.

"How about you go up to your room and wait for me there? I'll be right with you in a second."

"What are you going to do?" she asked, biting her lip, a look of concern across her face.

"Nothing, just gonna talk to Dad." He shrugged.

"Leave him be. He's sleeping."

"Jenny—"

"Please, don't wake him up. You're going to yell at each other, and I hate it when you do that." The girl's eyes were teary.

"What he did wasn't right, Jenny."

"He just forgot to go get me. You can't bother him for that. You know how distracted he is."

"That's no excuse. It's time for him to be responsible." She lowered her gaze to the floor as if he were scolding her. He put his hand under her sister's chin and raised her face gently. "I promise to play with you if you wait for me upstairs, okay?"

With nothing more to say, Jenny stomped up the stairs. He sighed and strolled to the sofa where John was.

Kevin looked at his father, or at least what was left of him, the shadow of the man he used to be, who Kevin had idolized so much in his childhood. John's unshaven cheek was glued to the stained sofa, his legs resting in a contorted manner as if he'd merely thrown himself on the couch, his hand on the floor beside an empty bottle.

Kevin knelt down, picked up the bottle, and noticed it had only a sip of alcohol left. He held the bottle over John's head and poured the cold drink on him. John jumped, his arms flailing.

"What the fuck?" the drunk man shouted, shaking his head.

"Are you serious?" Kevin asked. "What the hell is the matter with you?"

John sat up on the couch, trying to make sense of what was happening. He narrowed his eyes to see Kevin, and rubbed his temples.

"That's no way to talk to your father," he grunted.

"And this is not the way to treat your daughter," Kevin replied, taking a deep breath to keep from raising his voice. He did not want to scream. "I came home and found five messages on the answering machine. It was Jenny's teacher telling me you didn't go to pick her up. I decided to give you a chance. I thought that maybe you were looking for work, or that you were hired for a job you supposedly applied to. I wanted to have faith in you. I wanted to think that you would not leave your own daughter all by herself unless you had a very good reason."

"Look…"

"I don't want to hear your damn excuses."

"Kevin—"

"And what do I find when I get here? You passed out on the fucking couch with a hangover. What kind of example do you think you are setting for Jenny? Don't think about me. I can take care of myself. Think about her."

"Shit, Kevin, I'm sorry. I thought... I promise it won't happen again."

"Don't give me that shit!" Kevin yelled. "You've been saying that for months. Since Mom died, you've become a useless, parasitic prick. You think it's fair that I have to carry all of the responsibility? I bet you didn't even bother to look for a job."

"I'm on it," John replied. The black bags under his eyes made him look ten years older. "It's not easy, you know."

"Not if you spend the whole day drunk on some joint. We can't live off our savings forever, especially if you spend it all in booze."

"It's been hard for me, Kev," John said. He got up with difficulty and stretched, and all his bones protested. "Your mom was everything to me."

Kevin frowned. He could no longer contain his tears. "You are not the only one affected."

"I know," John confessed, opening his arms.

"No!" shouted Kevin, stepping aside. "We need you now more than ever, but you'd rather run away from your problems!"

Kevin went up to his room, ignoring the last words his father mumbled.

CHAPTER 6

James' torch could barely illuminate the massive, decaying house. The rotten walls showed the passing of time and abandonment. The sections in better condition were covered with graffiti that conveyed familiar messages, from insults and profanities to symbols like swastikas, pentagrams and some strange drawings that James couldn't decipher. They were memories of disturbed minds.

Black water dripped from the crumbling roof. The nauseating odor that flooded the abandoned place made the agent frown. The area was repulsive, all his senses told him to get out of there. James doubted that anyone in his right mind, criminal or not, could stay there for long.

According to the anonymous call they'd received, this place was used as a meeting place for selling drugs and, presumably, there had been recent activity. Cleyton thought it was just a waste of time, and kept his ass sit in his office as always. James had insisted that it was worth investigating anyway, but the lieutenant refused to go. After all, if it were somehow connected to the agent's theory, then Cleyton would do his best to move the investigation in the opposite direction.

"If you're so sure something is going on there, then go by yourself," the lieutenant had said. "If you see anything suspicious, call for backup."

"Asshole," James grumbled to himself. His voice echoed in the darkness.

He lowered the lantern's gaze to the ground to better see his path, full of debris and trash left over, taking each step with caution. If there were indeed anyone there, he had to be attentive to the slightest sound. At the moment, all he could hear was dripping coming from some rusty pipe.

In front of him, a dark corridor led to stairs going up to the second floor. To his left was an entryway to a completely empty room. To his right, there was a closed wooden door. James hesitated for a moment before going to his right and turning the handle. He put the flashlight on his belt and took out his revolver. He slowly pushed the door open as the rusty hinges chirped. Instinctively, he assumed combat position and raised the weapon.

The soft night air greeted him. The only thing in the room was a pair of torn mattresses and an open window whose blinds danced with the wind. James lowered his revolver with a sigh. He knew it had been a waste of time to come here. Maybe it might be best to return to the comfort of the station, but the case was going cold. Any chance, however small, had to be explored if he wanted to solve it. However…

Heavy footsteps echoed through the ceiling. Adrenaline shot through James' body, and he raised the revolver again with his eyes focused on any movement. He rushed into the darkness of the hallway and hurried up the stairs, skipping steps. On the second floor, the stench was even worse, as if dozens of dead animals had infected the place. His senses were alert. The muzzle of the gun pointed towards nothing.

"FBI! Whoever is in there, get out with your hands on the air!"

A rumble escaped from a bedroom at the end of the long corridor. The agent put a hand in his vest pocket, pulled out a portable radio, and hesitated for a moment. Truth be told, he didn't expect to find anyone there. That anonymous tip suddenly seemed too convenient to be true. His mind went blank for a second. Could it be a trap? If so, he had fallen right into it.

A shadow crossed the hallway from one room to another. James ran towards the shadow and, like a bull, struck open the wooden door with his shoulder. The impact ripped apart its hinges and raised a cloud of dust.

The black figure slid in the darkness. Instinctively, James pulled the trigger. One, two, three shots from the magnum lit the room for milliseconds. No bullet hit the suspect, who rushed to the window as if to take flight and jumped out.

James' heart stopped for a second. That crazy son of a bitch had just jumped from a second story window, almost twenty feet down. James ran and peered out the window, expecting to see an inert body on the pavement, but it was so dark he could barely discern a thing.

He hurried back the way he'd come, running down the stairs and venturing into the desolated street. The cold of the night received him with an embrace that gave him goosebumps. In the distance, a hooded figure ran away at an impressive speed, and James sprinted as fast as his legs allowed him, his feet barely touching the ground. The man glanced back over his shoulder to see his pursuer. The agent noticed a blue flash under the hoodie, with two huge black spots where his eyes should've been. The man was wearing a mask.

James placed his hand on his belt to get the revolver but hesitated. Any false move could kill the suspect and eliminate the only clue he had. Instead, he pulled the radio out of his pocket.

"I need backup! The suspect is wearing a black hoodie and a blue mask! He's going down the main avenue towards Bachman!" There was no response.

Before reaching the intersection, the masked man swerved to the left and plunged into the woods. James pressed the button on the radio.

"Damn it, Cleyton, send someone!"

James followed the suspect into the trees, his polished shoes buried deep in the mud with every quick step; he wasn't dressed for the occasion. James cursed his fate as he rushed into the vegetation.

36

Unable to see or hear anyone, he was sure he'd lost the guy. The man couldn't be far, but looking for him would be like trying to find a needle in a haystack.

The agent paused and did his best to sharpen his senses. All he could hear was the beating of his own heart. He raised the revolver, pointed up and pulled the trigger. The shot flew into the starry sky, releasing a flash of light that lasted less than a second and let out a deafening bang. To his right, the bushes shivered. He aimed the gun in that direction.

"Stop right now, or I'm going to shoot!" the agent shouted.

The man's silhouette zigzagged swiftly between the trees and went up a hill that returned to the street. Now James had him in sight. He continued his pursuit, his thighs screaming at every leap as he climbed the steep terrain until, at last, his feet trod on steady cement. He turned and clearly saw the hooded man running down the road. James spread his legs, put both hands on the hilt of the gun, took a long breath and held it, focused on the suspect. He couldn't fail. James took a shot. The bullet created a small cloud of smoke right next to the subject's legs, who kept on running.

"Crazy son of a bitch," James mumbled. He had purposely missed, hoping to scare the guy, but it didn't work.

As he prepared to fire again, the scream of police sirens pierced his ears. Red and blue lights blinked at the end of the street. A squad car appeared and stopped short, the wheels squealing. The masked man bounced off the hood of the vehicle and was thrown on the pavement. He got back up, stumbling.

"Get on your knees and put your hands behind your head!" James yelled as he approached, his gun pointed straight at the suspect's chest.

The hooded man obeyed. Two other officers got out of the car. One grabbed him by the wrists, pinned him against the hood and handcuffed him while the other came up to James and gave him a pat on the back. The agent wiped the sweat from his forehead while putting the revolver back in his holster. He'd had enough fun for the night.

The ride back to the station was quiet. James drove at a decent speed. The other two officers didn't even bother to wait for him, but that didn't matter; it was rather a relief. That way, he could take his time getting back to the station, maybe stop by at some fast food restaurant that was still open and relax.

His body was calm, but his mind kept repeating the events that had just occurred, as if his subconscious was trying to tell him something, to highlight a detail he might've overlooked. On the other hand, he was eager to see Cleyton's face. Perhaps now the lieutenant would take his proposals more seriously, but that was unlikely. Besides, there was Rudy. It would be irresponsible to pretend that everything was fine and celebrate a supposed victory that didn't even count as a clue. He wasn't going to waste his time like the rest of the useless people at the station. James stepped on the pedal. He had to interrogate the suspect as soon as possible.

By the time he arrived, the station was almost deserted, which wasn't surprising in the slightest. Most of the other officers would take any opportunity to avoid the paperwork that came with working in a police department, the kind of things that TV series and movies never showed.

Despite his irritation, he couldn't help but feel relieved that Cleyton had left. As much as James wanted to see the lieutenant swallow his own pride, the truth was that he would only be a hindrance. The best way to go about it would be for James to interrogate the suspect himself.

The agent went downstairs and found himself in front of Officer Reyes, who had been assigned to watch the cells that night.

"Step aside, Reyes."

The officer didn't move, he just stared at James, piercing the agent's skull with his gaze.

"Are you authorized?"

"I don't need to be authorized, I caught the guy myself."

"I only saw Smith and Velazquez bringing him. I didn't see you."

James' face reddened, and he clenched his fists until his nails stuck into the palm of his hand. Reyes was just giving him a hard time. As a FBI agent on a small-town police department, James could basically do as he pleased. The agent just walked past Reyes, bumping against his shoulder. Reyes didn't even bother following him. James reached the last cell where the masked man was supposed to be. The hooded figure that had given him such a hard time was only a boy, no older than twenty, sitting on the floor with his hood on top of his now naked face.

"Get up," said James to the young man. "I'll take you for a walk."

"How do you think you're going to get him out of there?" Reyes asked.

James raised his hand, holding a handful of keys. The officer's face paled as he put his hand on his belt where the keys should have been and opened his mouth to protest.

"The perks of being on the FBI," said James with a smile.

James tried three keys before finding the right one. He slid the iron door to the side and beckoned the boy forward. The kid obeyed, hands still cuffed and eyes fixed on the ground. James escorted him and threw the keys back at Reyes as he left. He heard a metallic clash on the floor behind him- Apparently, the officer didn't have very good reflexes.

James stepped into the poorly lit interrogation room. The only light source was an exposed bulb hanging from the ceiling. It wasn't supposed to intimidate or anything like that, it looked that way because of negligence, the place was falling apart. In the center was a wooden table with two chairs facing each other. James prepared to close the door behind him as soon as he saw the boy take a seat, however, someone stopped him before he could do so. The agent felt his heart skip a beat. He'd been so close.

He turned to see the last person he wanted to see, Cleyton. The lieutenant entered as if he owned the place, walking with his shoulders back and his head held high.

After an awkward silence, Cleyton finally said, "So you were about to have a little party and didn't care to invite me, huh?"

"I didn't see you when I arrived, so I assumed you were gone and didn't want to bother you until tomorrow," lied James.

"Well, now that you see it's no bother, catch me up."

James sighed.

"I went to the abandoned house. I found the suspect wearing a mask. He tried to flee so I chased him through the woods until Velazquez bumped into him and we were able to apprehend him. So far, the suspect hasn't spoken a single word."

Cleyton frowned as if he'd smelled shit. James thought that maybe if he took a shower every once in a while, he wouldn't have that face most of the time. The lieutenant reached into his vest and took out a plastic bag containing a few personal objects, including the mask and a wallet.

"We found an ID in his wallet," Cleyton said. He seemed to avoid looking at James directly. "The little thug is called Harry Sanders, no criminal record and graduated with honors from Heaven's Peak High School." The lieutenant's attention went straight to the guy. "Tell me a little about yourself, Harry, what were you doing in the middle of the night in an abandoned house?"

Sanders just looked at his own reflection in the mirror in front of him, unresponsive.

"There's no one back there," said Cleyton, as if reading the guy's thoughts. "It's just us."

There was only silence for a good couple of minutes, the tension thick on the air. Harry Sanders didn't blink once.

"You were going to see someone," said James. "A dealer, or maybe a client." The agent leaned on the table with both hands; he wanted Sanders to look at him. "I think it would do you good to spend some time in the cell, you know, to clear your mind. Loosen up the tongue."

"I did nothing wrong," Sanders said at last. His voice was monotonous, and each word carried the cold of winter. "You can't arrest me for taking a night walk."

"Trespassing," said James calmly. "That house is private property."

"It's funny though," said Sanders, whose gaze was still dead as a corpse. "I didn't see you arresting any of the homeless people who sleep there."

"There was nobody else there," James replied. He was starting to lose patience. "Besides, I'm sure none of them would be wearing a mask. What I ask myself is why a mask? Why you would want to hide your identity unless you were planning to do something illegal? But I caught you before you did it or you had already done it by the time I arrived."

"You didn't catch me. Your cop friends did," Sanders said.

Cleyton chuckled. The blood rose on James' face.

"I think that what you were doing in that place is pretty clear," James said. "My only question is: Who were you going to meet?"

The silence returned. James waited a couple of minutes with his eyes fixed on Sanders. He had to make him feel pressured.

"This is a waste of time," growled Cleyton.

Sanders's eyes dodged over James's, only for a split second, and went down to his lap. James noticed that the guy had his hands under the table. The agent stood up and walked around the room. Sanders' hands rested on his lap, specifically, in his front pockets.

"Where did you find the ID?" James asked.

"In his wallet." Cleyton shrugged.

"Which was in..."

"His jacket."

"So you didn't check his pockets."

Sanders' face turned white, his eyes widened, and they went straight to the lieutenant.

"Son of a bitch," Cleyton said.

James took a few steps toward the boy, who jumped out of his chair, his hands shaking without leaving his thighs, trying to protect his secret. Sanders stepped back slowly until his back hit the wall, cornered.

"You're just making it harder for yourself," said James, his hands raised. "Let me propose something to you. If you cooperate, you'll have all the protection we can give you. How does that sound? You don't have to fear retaliation from whomever you are working with. The only thing you have to do is tell us what you know."

"Come on, spit it out," said Cleyton.

As if accepting his fate, Harry Sanders put his skeletal hand in his pocket and took out a small flask. Inside, there was a purple substance, almost black. If it weren't for the color, James would have sworn it was blood.

He'd heard rumors about a drug on the streets, something new and exotic that had never been seen before. To tell the truth, he didn't expect the boy to have anything more than a little marijuana or some cocaine at best. This was totally different. He was sure they'd hit the jackpot.

What happened next lasted only a fraction of a second. Cleyton's fist struck Sander's face, and the guy fell backward on the floor. The flask rolled to the other side of the room. Before James could react, the lieutenant lifted Harry by his T-shirt and threw him on the table like a rag doll.

"What the fuck are you doing?" James yelled.

"Giving this little shit what he deserves," Cleyton replied, punching Sanders in his stomach.

"Stop!"

"I'll do whatever you want," Harry begged, his face contorted into a grimace of terror and pain.

Cleyton threw him to the ground.

"This is unacceptable!" James yelled.

"What's unacceptable is this piece of garbage walking my streets," Cleyton replied.

"You're not going to kick a confession out of him." James grabbed Cleyton by the shoulder, but the lieutenant pushed him into the wall.

James felt a throbbing pain run through his spine as he let out a grunt. He leaned his hand against the wall to keep his balance. His fingers slipped instinctively around his waist, where his dear revolver rested. He felt tempted to take it out and empty the cartridge into Cleyton's skull but resisted.

"The sheriff is going to find out about this," James said.

"Fuck the sheriff," Cleyton said as he kicked the boy's ribs.

James threw himself at the door. Like a storm, he made his way down the aisle and entered Gordon's office, where he found Gordon chatting happily on the phone, leaning back in his chair with both feet on the desk. James slammed the door behind him, and the sheriff's smile turned into a grimace.

"Cleyton is kicking the shit out of a suspect!" James shouted.

"I'll call you in a second, Brian," said the sheriff before hanging up. His tone was too calm. "Agent, sometimes you have to break a few eggs, you know what I mean?"

"This has gone too far!" James snapped. "There is a law, a procedure to carry out in situations like these."

"Don't come to me with hypocrisies, Agent. I'm sure the FBI has done worse things to accomplish their goals."

"I've seen things that I wish I hadn't, but those have been cases of very dangerous people with all the evidence to prove their guilt. This is just a boy who could actually help us go further."

"If so, then does it matter how you get this information?"

"Damn it," James spat, outraged. "You're all insane."

He returned to the interrogation room with his heart in his throat. Harry's face was soaked with red, blood dripping into his eyes from a wound on his forehead. Cleyton, for his part, had only his fists painted, and a murderous look fixed on the boy. James pulled the revolver out of his belt and pointed it at the lieutenant.

"Stop right fucking now," James commanded.

Cleyton stood paralyzed for a second.

"The dog does bite," he said with a smile on his face.

Cleyton swiftly pulled out his 9mm from his jacket and aimed the pistol between James' eyebrows. He took the safety off the gun, which clicked and echoed in the empty room.

"This will cost you your badge," James said, trying to sound calm.

"And it's going to cost *you* your head if you don't leave right now," Cleyton replied.

Both stood in place, facing each other with guns raised. Harry Sanders crawled on the floor and grabbed the flask he'd dropped. Cleyton shifted the gun barrel towards Sanders.

"Don't even think about it," Cleyton ordered.

But it was too late. Harry removed the cap and drank the viscous liquid in one gulp. Cleyton cursed and put his finger on the trigger. James jumped over the lieutenant and swung his arm up. The bullet came out and opened a hole in the ceiling. They both collapsed on the floor. Harry started shouting and laughing, a maniacal laugh that spread throughout the police station. Cleyton pushed James aside and stood up. Just then, Harry spat a black substance into Cleyton's face. The lieutenant covered his face with both hands as if he'd been hit with boiling water.

"Son of a bitch!"

Several officers appeared, alert, with their pistols in hand. Among them was Sheriff Gordon, shoving them aside to make his way in. His face was paper-white and sweat poured from his forehead.

"Enough!" he yelled. "I'm sick of your childish shit! You could've killed someone!" He waved to one of the officers. "Reyes, take the suspect to the cell."

James struggled to his feet, brushed the dust off his suit and adjusted his tie. Reyes grabbed Harry Sanders by the elbow and pulled him out of the room.

"As for the two of you," said Gordon to James and Cleyton. "Get out of my station, I don't want to see either of you here until you've calmed the fuck down."

The lieutenant went out like a beast. James buttoned his vest before retiring. Outside, Sanders was still laughing as they carried him to his cell.

CHAPTER 7

None of the students in the classroom paid any attention to what the teacher was saying. Everyone took refuge in their own thoughts while eagerly waiting for the bell to ring. Yet the teacher kept talking, too absorbed in his own speech to realize he was talking to himself.

Kevin stared out the window with his chin resting on his hand. He could almost feel the breeze outside. A fleeting movement passed through his field of vision, and he glimpsed a piece of paper submitted to the will of the wind. It contained a picture of a smiling child with huge letters reading: MISSING. Kevin felt a twist in his stomach and looked away. He couldn't begin to imagine how terrible it must be to lose a loved one in such a horrible way, not knowing where they were or even if they were okay.

Kevin tried to focus on something else, anything that could distract him. He looked around the room; most of the faces were already familiar. After two weeks, it was expected that he'd know their names as well, but, after all, he'd always been the solitary type. He focused on himself and his art. He liked it that way, which was why he didn't have that many friends; he had that in common with his sister. By then, anyone else would know by heart the names of their classmates, but he barely remembered a handful, those with whom he had spoken at some point or whose names were easy to remember.

Of course, there were exceptions. Like Rob Jensen, also known as the teachers' nightmare, a filthy-looking boy who made life miserable for everyone. He wasn't very tall or muscular, but he had a piercing gaze that could intimidate anyone. Kevin remembered a rumor he'd heard, that Rob supposedly had a confrontation with one of the teachers. Legend had it that the argument came about because Rob kept skipping classes and his teacher wanted to send him to the principal's office, and then things got out of hand when Rob struck the teacher with his skateboard. The teacher ended up hospitalized, and Rob was suspended for a while. Kevin had only seen him a couple of times. Luckily, the guy didn't come to school all that much.

To his right sat a blonde girl with folded arms and eyes glued to her empty desk. Her name was Sofia Everett. He remembered her because she was the sister of the boy who had recently gone missing. Everyone talked about her the first few days Kevin had arrived, some with sympathy, and others with morbid curiosity. He knew that she was the best in almost every class, an outstanding student. However, during all the time he'd been there, he never saw her take notes or raise her hand to answer any of the teacher's questions. She just stared at her desk, inert as a statue. Kevin sometimes wondered if the girl was still breathing. Then, the bell would ring, and she was always the first to leave.

He must've done something this time to give some hint that he was watching her because the girl's head suddenly turned to him. Kevin tried dodging her gaze a second too late.

The bell rang. The teacher continued talking to himself as the students left the classroom. By the time Kevin had gathered enough courage to turn to his right, Sofia was gone.

"I didn't know you liked her," said a voice behind him. It was one of his classmates, Jessica. Kevin had asked for her notes to catch up with the others. Jessica had a grin on her face. "I don't think you have a chance with her. Not because you're ugly but, well, I've known her for a long time, and I've never heard of her having a boyfriend."

"I'm not interested in her," said Kevin.

"Oh, really? Because I saw you looking at her with puppy eyes." Jessica's smile widened.

"What? No... just... I was thinking how horrible it must've been for her, you know? With her brother missing and all."

The smile vanished from Jessica's face. "Oh, well, yes, I guess you're right. Anyway, changing to a less depressing subject, that's not the reason I wanted to talk to you. You see, the senior students are having a party this weekend, and I was wondering if you wanted to stop by."

"What's the catch?"

"There's no catch. How can you think that about me?" Jessica asked, pretending to be offended. Kevin raised an eyebrow. "Okay, alright, you caught me. You like to take pictures, don't you? I was wondering if maybe you'd like to bring your camera and take a couple of pictures."

"Well, I mean, I don't know," Kevin replied, trying to come up with an excuse.

"Please! Come on! I already told the guys I knew someone who would do us the favor."

"Didn't you think to ask me first?"

"Yes, and I'm sorry, but my friends and I really want, no, we *need* to go to that party. Pretty please? They said they would pay you for the pictures."

"Are you serious? They're willing to pay me?" Kevin found himself suddenly interested.

"Yes, so even if you get bored, you wouldn't be wasting your time because you'd be earning some extra cash. What do you say? Please say yes."

"I'll have to think about it. My dad likes to go out on weekends, so I have to stay at home and take care of my sister."

"You think your dad will go out this Saturday?"

"I don't know, he said he wouldn't," Kevin remembered the argument they had and didn't know whether to believe his father's promise.

"Then, I don't see the problem. Can't you talk to him?"

That was not exactly an option with John. Anything Kevin told him would go in one ear and out the other. He thought about Jenny. They might need some extra money if John was still wasting all he had on booze.

"Well, I could use some cash," he said, sighing deeply. "Okay, I'll do it. You're a good saleswoman."

Jessica laughed, jumping with joy.

"You're my hero! I'll see you on Saturday then." She took a piece of paper out of her pocket and handed it to Kevin. "This is the address. Don't lose it! And thanks again. Seriously, you're the best."

Jessica walked away, making heart figures with her fingers. Kevin could not help but smile.

CHAPTER 8

The desk was a pile of garbage, a fine example of an artist's mind, scattered and chaotic but with a proper order out of which only its owner could make sense. There were two empty cans of energy drinks on one side, a pair of open notebooks and dozens of photographs spread all over the surface. Kevin had tried to sort them somehow, by category, theme or something, but it was difficult. They all told their own story and conveyed a unique feeling. He leaned back in his chair, his room now feeling lonelier than ever.

Outside the window, trees lined the streets and their red and orange foliage covered the roofs of the other houses down the hill. It was a beautiful view but, strangely enough, he had never taken a picture of it. The truth was that, no matter how good the artist, the work could never faithfully portray the beauty of nature.

Some of the photographs would have the privilege of being hung on the wall, but he had to take one last look to be sure. After deep consideration, he decided to divide them into two columns. The Winners one, reserved for the pictures chosen to be on the wall, and the Losers one, reserved for photos whose destiny was to be kept in the drawer of memories.

To his left lay a picture of the green mountains at sunset, taken the day of his arrival in Heaven's Peak. He put that one in the Winners section. Another one had his father carrying the sofa towards the living room with the help of some neighbor. That one went straight to the Losers pile.

The next picture showed Jenny on the swings in the park. The colors seemed to jump out of the image and take on a life of their own. He expected the breeze to sway the branches of the trees and the girl to come to life as if it were a movie. A smile appeared on his face. He couldn't remember the last time he'd seen her so happy. He decided the picture deserved to be on the wall of fame.

However, just before throwing it with the other winners, he took one last look. Something wasn't right. He squinted and brought the photo closer. The forest behind his sister was so thick that the branches mingled with one another. Amidst the shadows, a humanoid figure stood, imposing, camouflaged, almost invisible. Kevin remembered the feeling of being watched at the time and felt his heart pumping in his chest.

He searched through the rest of the pictures. Perhaps he would find a second one of that day, one that proved what he saw was just an optical illusion. There had to be one. He swallowed and hoped for the best as he swept the desk with his arm, tossing the cans and notebooks to the floor. Kevin divided the photos as best he could, his gaze fleeting over each one, desperate. A bead of cold sweat slid down his forehead.

Then he found it, hidden among the Losers group. Half of Jenny's torso was cut from the frame, as his main subject wasn't her but the woods behind her. He took a detailed look at it for a few seconds, straining his eyes. There it was, he was sure of it now. That shadow was a person, or at least it looked like one. Its limbs were monstrously long, its height comparable with that of the trees around it, and where its face was supposed to be there was only white as if it was wearing a mask.

Kevin's heart pounded faster, and a knot in his stomach made him feel dizzy. He had heard the stories, had seen the missing people's posters. Was somebody stalking them? According to rumors, the most recent victims had been children. He had to talk to Jenny, if she had seen anything, then he would call the police.

He snuck into his sister's room. Jenny lay on her belly, drawing, surrounded by colorful papers that covered the whole floor like a carpet. He looked out over the sea of artwork, and the tones gradually darkened.

The first drawings showed children playing, suns, rainbows and joyful landscapes. However, as he looked the more recent ones, they started to lose their liveliness. The warm colors became increasingly colder. In one section, most were nothing but shades of red and black.

His photographs often reflected his moods, his feelings. When his mother passed away, the scenes he captured were melancholic, solitary and crude. He hadn't even noticed it until his father said something about it. He couldn't even see those photographs anymore, for they sunk him into a sea of sadness, a darkness that his heart refused to feel again.

He wondered if his sister was dealing with her pain in the same way.

"Hey, booger, can I come in?" Kevin asked.

"No, you can't come in until you've given me a million dollars," said Jenny with a sly smile.

"Wow, a million dollars. That's a pricey ticket. I hope it's worth the investment."

"Of course, you have permission to see my art collection. You have to take advantage now before I'm famous and sell all my paintings."

Kevin laughed. Maybe his sister was quieter than before, but her personality hadn't changed at all. He threw himself at her, grabbing her by her armpits and raising her over his head. He had to enjoy those little moments now before she grew so much that he could no longer lift her. He kissed her on the cheek.

"Have you changed the style of your art or what? I remember your drawings being more colorful, brighter," said Kevin.

"Uh, well, it's better to use dark colors. The lighter ones look like candy but can't be eaten." Jenny's gaze wandered around the room as if she did not want her eyes to meet Kevin's.

"You tried to eat them, didn't you?" Kevin asked with a smile.

"I don't know," Jenny replied with a shrug.

Kevin laughed. He was tempted to forget the reason he had come to visit and enjoy the moment, but he had to insist. He was afraid Jenny wasn't completely honest. She always avoided looking at him when she lied.

"Don't you like my drawings?" Jenny asked with puppy eyes.

"Of course I like them! You're an artist! Who wouldn't like your drawings?" Kevin asked, putting her back on the floor. "I'm just saying, because, well, I've noticed that you've changed the way you draw. That happens sometimes. Art is a window to our feelings. That's why I've also changed my style a couple of times, depending on how I felt at the time. I guess what I want to ask you is: how do you feel?"

"Oh!" Jenny looked surprised at the question. "Good, I guess. School is boring."

"As every school should be."

"But I have a good time when I get home. I can sit and draw whenever I want, and I get to have fun with you," Jenny concluded.

"And all you do is draw when I'm not around?"

"Yeah, why? What's wrong with that?"

"Nothing, nothing at all, silly. It's just that, you know, I talked to your teacher the other day."

"She says I should hang out with the other kids," Jenny snorted with frustration.

"It's okay if you don't want to do it. You can focus on your art. Besides, I'd be jealous, you might enjoy playing with them more than with me."

"That's impossible," said Jenny grinning.

Kevin grinned back. His gaze fell on one of the drawings. It was the sketch of a child holding hands with a black-suited figure. The boy looked sad, even frightened. The man in black, on the other side, didn't seem to have features on his face. That reminded him of the reason why he was there.

"Who is he?"

"I don't know, the boogeyman, I guess? I've dreamed about him a lot," Jenny answered.

"What are the dreams like?"

"They're like nightmares. I don't remember them very well, I just wake up scared at night." Kevin's heart shrank. "When I draw him the nightmares stop, so I do it often, but then it gets worse because I have to do more and more."

"Why didn't you tell me that, Jenny?"

"I thought you would say they are children's things. Grown-ups always say that."

"Well, I'm not a grown-up. I'm your brother, and no matter what, I'll be by your side to protect you, okay?"

Jenny nodded as she hugged her brother. Kevin gathered the courage to ask.

"That man, the boogeyman, do you know him?"

Jenny jerked away from him in bewilderment. "No, I've never seen him."

Kevin sighed with relief, not noticing that his sister had avoided his gaze when she answered.

CHAPTER 9

⌒

The historical documents of Heaven's Peak didn't show anything relevant. James had been hoping to find a clue, some event related to the disappearances. The newspapers on his desk stared back at him silently. All he saw were some news articles that showed the families of the victims at their most vulnerable moment, nothing more. He had been awake all night, searching the files on the case. He had managed to put together a list of all the victims' relatives. Perhaps someone would have something to say, something that had been overlooked by his incompetent coworkers, but it was unlikely.

James threw all the papers to the floor with a grunt. He rubbed his eyes and looked at his watch. It had been an hour since his last cup of coffee, his fifth to be exact, and he craved the next. He ran a hand over his face to wake up and got up. He had an idea.

He dragged his feet to the door and put his ear against it. Nothing. It was lunchtime, so there shouldn't be many officers hanging around. Gordon had been a pain in the ass since the interrogation with Sanders. After what had happened, it was to be expected. What that fat idiot didn't understand was that they could not waste any more time, for every second that passed was a second less in the life of that child. It was better to sneak into the cells and try to convince Reyes to let him through than having to deal with whatever shit Gordon threw at him.

He crept down the hall like a cat, looking over his shoulder to make sure no one noticed his presence. He heard voices coming from another hallway. Quickly, he turned his back on the voices and pretended to be drinking water from the fountain. The two men walked past behind him, engrossed in their conversation. Once he was sure that he was alone again, he resumed his journey, crossing the corner to the other corridor and going down the stairs to the cells.

Reyes was reading a book in his chair. When he noticed the agent's presence, he jumped as if he'd been caught with his pants down. James saw that what was inside the book was a pornographic magazine.

"What a sophisticated piece of literature you have in your hand, Reyes," James said. "I guess if I hadn't come you'd have the other hand in your crotch. "

"What the fuck are you doing down here?" Reyes growled.

"Do you have a family, Officer?"

"What does that have to do with anything?"

"Just a simple question, Officer. Tell me, are you married?"

"A wife and two daughters, why do you care?" Reyes replied.

"I care a lot. It's the reason why I'm in this line of work. To serve and protect. Not you, you seem capable of defending yourself, but people like your family, innocent people that want to lead their lives in peace."

"Don't come up with bullshit."

"I come from a humble background, Officer," James interrupted. "My mother was a full-time housewife and my father, may he rest in peace, was an officer of the law, just like you. My mother was religious. She used to go to church every Sunday and had a table in the living room dedicated exclusively to the Bible. Every night, before bed, I would kneel with her to pray. Sometimes, I would thank God, others I would wish for world peace, but most of the time I would ask that my father came home safely every night." Reyes kept silent. He seemed to be trying to guess where James was going with his speech. "I don't know if it worked. I do know that every night my father came home, safe and sound. My mother said it was thanks to a divine being who listened to our prayers and answered them. When I asked my father, he told me that it was thanks to people like him, heroes who put their lives at risk on a daily basis to help others, to maintain order and ensure compliance with the law. That's why I am where I am, Officer. Because I believe in my father's words."

"B-But the Sheriff—"

"Look at me, Reyes, look me in the eyes," James ordered, facing him. "That missing child, Rudy Everett, is in danger, and any one of your daughters may be next. Do you understand what I'm saying? I don't have time for formalities and stupid shit like that. That guy in the cells behind you is the only clue we have to get to the bottom of this." The officer shook his head without looking up. "Think of your daughters. Don't you want them to grow up in a safe place? In a place where you don't have to be looking over your shoulder in the middle of the day?"

"If I let you in, I risk losing my badge," said Reyes. "If that happens, I won't be able to provide for my family. So, I am thinking of them when I tell you that I cannot let you in. Besides, what do you even know about having a family?"

"Not much," admitted James. "I was about to have one. I had a wife. We spent two years trying to have children, and we had three miscarriages. We went to several doctors, and they all told us the same thing. It was highly unlikely that we could ever have children. She committed suicide a few months after that."

The silence reigned for long and heavy seconds until Reyes rose from his chair, looked through his keys and opened the metallic door that led to the cells.

"Five minutes. Shit, I cannot believe I'm doing this..."

"You're doing God's work, Reyes." James patted him on the shoulder.

James crossed the threshold, looking everywhere. Most of the cells were empty. The lamps gave the place a dingy atmosphere with their dim light. The cold seemed concentrated, like a refrigerator. Until that moment he hadn't noticed that winter was coming.

Sanders was in the last cell on the left. A thread of red liquid slid between the bars. James stopped short. He wanted to call Reyes, but the words stayed in his mouth. He stepped forward and leaned in to see the inside of the cell

"Damn it," he whispered.

Sanders lay on the floor, his body contorted in a pool of his own blood, with his head smashed open. Bits of brains were scattered alongside ceramic fragments of what used to be the sink. One of his eyes peered out as if it wanted to free itself from its basin.

James felt lightheaded, his stomach threatening to return the five cups of coffee he'd had. After all of his years of service in the FBI, he had grown used to seeing dead bodies, but none of them had gotten under his skin like this one. Reyes rose abruptly at the sight of the agent's pale face.

"What is it?" he asked. His voice seemed to come from miles away.

"Call for help," James said.

Reyes ran to the agent and cursed when he saw Sanders' open skull. The officer pulled the radio from his belt and reported the scene. James leaned his back against the wall and slid down to sit on the floor. In a matter of seconds, most of the station had come down. A crowd of police officers surrounded Sanders' cell, speculating with a mixture of morbidity and uncertainty of how such a thing could have happened.

James had no answer for that. It was impossible for anyone to mock the security of the police station and enter the cells without anyone noticing. Who would go to all that work just to silence the boy? Unless…

"The crazy son of a bitch committed suicide," exclaimed Cleyton on arrival.

"Do you really think that?" James asked.

"The other option is for someone to get into the police station in the middle of the night and kill him," the lieutenant said. It was the first time James heard him speak in such a calm tone. "But that doesn't sound very likely."

"There is a third option," James said as he rose from the floor and brushed off his pants. All the officers around him stared at him. James adjusted his suit and cleared his throat before continuing. "Somebody working in the station killed him."

CHAPTER 10

Rob Jensen spat in the sink. His saliva was red again. He turned on the faucet, filled his hands with cold water and cleaned his face as if that would magically heal his wounds. It wouldn't, but it eased the pain a little. He wiped off his face cautiously and waited a few seconds to arm himself with enough courage to look at his reflection. A red stripe crossed his forehead, reaching down his eyebrow. He took a closer look at it and ruled out the possibility of needing stitches.

The young man that looked back at him in the mirror was pathetic, for a teenager he already had a thick beard that would make a thirty-year-old jealous. His brown eyes had a cold, cutting look, and his long, brown hair was a mess; he might even be missing a few strands after what his father had done to him.

A sudden hatred flared inside Rob. With a roar, he struck the mirror with his bare fist. The glass shattered, pieces stuck in his knuckles. That gave him some pleasure, the self-inflicted pain. It was the kind of pain that had a purpose, unlike the suffering caused by another, which was erratic and abusive.

"Is everything all right, sweetheart?" asked a trembling female voice on the other side of the door.

"Yeah, Mom," Rob replied, his fists clenched so tightly that pieces of glass slipped from the wounds.

"You need to put on some alcohol. Please, open up. I'll help you."

"No."

"It's in the upper cabinet, to the right."

"I know." He knew it too well.

Rob opened the door and saw his mother's thin, decrepit face. Margery was in her thirties, but she looked two decades older. Her black hair fell on her shoulders like a burned waterfall. She had bags under her eyes and scratches on her face. She covered her mouth with her bony hands, exposing old bruises that were now green spots on her arms. Rob never got used to that image, no matter how many times he saw it. As a child, it broke his heart but now, almost a man, it made his blood boil.

"Oh, my God," she mumbled. "What did you do?"

"Stop acting like you care about me," said Rob, pushing her out of the way.

"Of course I do, sweetie."

"Shut up!" Rob yelled. "Just shut up. You can stop lying, Mom. I know you don't give a fuck about me. I can live with that. I can accept that. What I cannot stand is that you insist on trying to prove something that's not true, like I'm some kind of idiot."

"Oh, my Robbie."

"Don't call me that."

"I love you more than—"

"If you loved me, you would've done something."

She shook her head and stared at the floor, covering her mouth to keep from sobbing.

"What do you want me to do?" she finally asked. "It's not like I have a chance against him, and you remember what happened when we called the police, don't you?"

"Those assholes don't give a fuck about anyone either."

"Sweetheart, your daddy loves us. He just—he has a bad temper, and we have to learn to deal with that."

"Where is he?" Rob asked as if he hadn't heard her.

"He's on the couch. He wanted to watch television."

"Shit."

"Why?"

"None of your business," said Rob, leaving and slamming the door behind him.

Rob went downstairs. Darkness shrouded the room with the exception of a light coming from the small television resting on a shelf. The colors flickered incessantly around the room. Jack's snore obscured the noise from the TV. The sofa was stuck to the wall so he couldn't see clearly where that asshole was.

Rob swallowed. His heart throbbed as if it would come out of his chest at any moment. If all the yelling upstairs didn't wake up his father, then nothing else would, but still...

With a knot in his stomach, Rob slid his feet through the carpet. He inhaled as deeply as he could and held his breath. He was tempted to grab the remote and turn off the television, to be hidden in the dark in case his father woke up, but that would leave him blind as well.

Slowly, he made his way through the room, eyes fixed on his feet, deciding with caution where to step. The wooden floor creaked under the rug, and Rob turned to his father. The silhouette on the couch didn't move. That relieved him, but the fact that Jack had stopped snoring worried him. Rob stayed, petrified, his legs begging him to run.

"Rob, please!" Margery shouted from the stairs.

Jack rose from the couch and growled with frustration. "I can't catch some sleep in this fucking house!"

Rob ran to the front door and threw himself into the street. A tug on his shirt pulled him back and made him crash against the floor. There was Jack. Big, tall and wide, with a murderous look, thirsty for blood. Rob crawled back to the living room and got up without taking his eyes off the mole in front of him.

"Please don't hurt him," Margery begged.

"I'm not gonna hurt him," Jack said. "I'm gonna kill him."

The blow went straight to Rob's cheek. His head jerked to the side and into the ground. Jack grabbed Rob by the feet and dragged him across the floor. Rob kicked as hard as he could, all of his efforts focused on releasing his legs. He finally managed to set one free and, with deadly precision, kicked his father in the groin.

The man fell to his knees with a howl. Rob stood up like a shot and ran into the street. Behind him came the smell of beer and sweat along with screaming and cursing.

Rob jumped the fence into the neighbor's backyard. For a second, he wondered if his father would follow him that far and figured that Jack was more likely to try to run through the fence than jump over it. His sprint turned into a trot and then a brisk walk until he reached the main avenue, where a dead silence reigned. A chilly breeze made its way into Rob's bones. The clothes he was wearing made no difference. It was as if he were walking naked out in the open. He took a cigarette and lighter from his pocket. He tried to light it several times until it finally gave birth to a small flame. A momentary relief ran through his body with each puff he took, but he still wasn't completely relaxed.

It took him a moment to notice that he was at George Hellen's Plaza. At that hour of the night there wasn't a single soul around, which was a shame considering that no more than a couple of years ago, people would gather around the plaza to have some drinks and chat all night. At the time it was like a weekend tradition. Now, everyone was so afraid to leave their houses after dark that people would rather spend the night in someone else's home than at one of the few clubs in town and wait for the sunrise, so their way back home would be safer.

Rob walked around and stopped in front of George Hellen's statue; he was a mayor from the early sixties who had turned Heaven's Peak into a resort town, introducing tourism as a source of income. Since its founding, Heaven's Peak had been a mining town, but that ended in 1962 when a coal mine fire scared the whole community and it was decided to cease all activity. Everyone thought the economy was going to decline, but good ol' George avoided the catastrophe and people's quality of life actually improved. The guy deserved his place of honor.

Even so, the statue disturbed Rob. It was as if those bronze eyes could follow him wherever he went. He looked at his wristwatch. It was twenty minutes past midnight. Anybody else in town would have told him he was crazy for being out so late. Rob preferred that to have to face his father. He sighed, hoping the old man would forget what had happened tonight after he dealt with tomorrow's hangover, but he doubted it.

Rob stood there for another half hour, breathing in the night air. A creak behind him made him jump out of his trance. The tree branches clashed with one another, waving in the soft breeze. He didn't know exactly why, but it made all the hairs on his body stand on end. Rob sat at the foot of the statue, alert to any movement around him, no matter how small.

The sound of footsteps echoed on the empty night. He sprang up and turned. Just a few feet away from him, a man dressed in black was hiding under the shadow of a tree. The only thing Rob could discern was his silhouette.

"I can see you, dumbass!" Rob yelled. He took a deep puff of the cig and let the smoke come out with his words. "Who do you think you're scaring?"

The man approached slowly as if calculating every move. Rob was tempted to step back but kept his feet planted firmly on the ground. As the man in black came closer, more of his appearance was revealed. Rob narrowed his eyes. The man was wearing black, and somehow didn't seem to have any features. In fact, the man's face was covered by a mask with two black spots where his eyes were supposed to be. It seemed as though the mask was attached to his face, or rather as if it were part of his skin. Rob felt a growing uneasiness as the man got closer.

"You can stay right there," Rob shouted. The masked man continued his approach. Now Rob could see him perfectly under the streetlights. "I'm warning you."

The man in black was now just a few feet away from him. Rob finally took a few steps back; his legs seemed to have a mind of their own. The masked man stopped at last, barely inches away from his face. Rob inhaled one last time as he dropped the cigarette butt and stepped on it. He spat a gray cloud at the grim mask.

"You have nothing to say? Or are you a mute?" Rob said defiantly, his heart pounding.

The masked man put his index finger where his lips were supposed to be, signaling for Rob to be quiet. The hairs on the back of Rob's neck bristled. The stranger put his hand on his jaw as if to remove his mask and pulled. It came off as if it were ripping off his own skin. Rob listened to the viscous sound as the mask lifted, revealing what lay beneath, something he instantly regretted seeing.

Rob screamed as loud as he could. The stranger vomited a black substance on Rob's face. It was unbearable, as if a jar of acid were searing his face. He put both hands to his face, shrieking in pain as he fell and writhed on the ground.

His eyes were on fire. His throat began to itch, then to burn. In just a few seconds, he felt as if he had drunk gasoline and swallowed a lighter. The pain ran through his body, burning him from the inside out. Rob convulsed, shaking and moving from side to side as if engulfed in flames.

The last thing he saw before losing consciousness were those black, cold eyes, watching him.

CHAPTER 11

⟨~⟩

The light of the camera flashed Jessica and her friends, who posed together making funny faces. Kevin took several more pictures, at different angles and positions. He took the girls to almost every corner of that mansion. The place seemed endless, full of people who drank, danced and chatted happily. Just because of the place's size and the sheer number of people, Kevin thought they must have invited the whole town. He asked the girls to stand by the food table and improvise. The girls posed pretending to fight for a piece of cake. Kevin was surrounded by delicious food and beautiful girls; he couldn't be happier. The girls blinked after being blinded by the flash. Jessica staggered over to her photographer and kissed him on the cheek.

"Thank you for coming," she said, inches from his ear.

He smiled back at her and thanked himself for going to the party.

"Your glass is still full. Don't you drink?" Jessica asked, raising her voice over the music.

"Of course," lied Kevin with a mischievous grin. "I just try not to get too dizzy while I take the pictures."

Jessica poked her temple with her finger. "Genius, but it's time to have some fun."

She grabbed the plastic cup resting on the table, placed it between his fingers and guided it to his lips. Kevin hesitated for a moment, unsure. He closed his eyes and drank it all in one gulp. The bitter taste poisoned his tongue and made him frown. Jessica and the girls around burst into laughter while clapping and jumping. Kevin had the decency to blush.

"You see, it's not so bad, is it?" Jessica chirped.

"I guess not. I still don't understand why people like it so much."

"Take a couple more drinks, then you'll know."

"I see your intentions, Jess. I won't let you get me drunk and take advantage of me."

Jessica lowered her gaze to the floor and back up to him. She seemed to be present and absent at the same time. Kevin supposed that the alcohol was starting to have an effect on the girl, or on him.

"You're a dick," she said, giving him a gentle push on the shoulder.

Kevin laughed and took a glance around the room. The group had split up into couples that were talking or dancing. He couldn't help but notice someone's absence.

"What happened to that girl? The blonde one." Kevin asked. Jessica looked at him strangely. "You know, the one with the missing brother."

"Oh." Her smile faded in an instant. "Why do you ask me about her?"

"I don't know." Kevin shrugged. "It just seems strange she's not here. You're friends, right?"

"Yes, I guess... I mean, we're not that close. Besides, she's still trying to get over the thing with her brother."

"That must be horrible. I don't know what I would do if..."

He didn't even want to imagine the possibility of something like that happening to Jenny. Then he remembered the figure, the one he saw watching them from the woods. His sister had avoided looking him in the eye when he asked her about it. Such a small but significant detail he had overlooked at the time. Kevin's heartbeat stopped for a second. He grabbed another cup from a nearby table and swallowed it whole

"Are you okay?" Jessica asked.

"No," Kevin replied, turning around. "I have to go."

"You can't go," she said, grabbing him by the shoulder. "You just got here."

"Two hours ago."

"Exactly."

He looked at her in confusion. "I have to go back to my sister," Kevin said after a pause.

"She'll be fine," she assured. "You said your dad would take care of her, you have nothing to worry about."

You don't know my father.

"Sorry, Jess, really."

"Please, don't go," Jessica begged. "Who will take our pictures? Besides, it's dangerous to be walking around town by yourself in the middle of the night."

"Tell Dave I had an emergency. I'll give him the pictures I took and tell him not to worry about the pay."

She gave him an annoyed look and stomped her foot. Her nails dug into Kevin's arm. He pulled his arm away from her, and his elbow struck someone coming with a tray of glasses, which fell to the ground in a waterfall of liquor. A girl somewhere shrieked and, after that, silence fell over the room. Blood rose to his face in shame. He apologized, glanced quickly at Jessica, and headed to the exit.

Later, on his restless nights, Kevin would try to relive those memories, again and again, looking for answers, only to find blurred images that would intertwine with each other without any meaning.

The streetlights were nothing more than a faint glow, weak as a candle, the sidewalk was almost invisible at his feet, and the cold wind pierced his bones. His head felt light, dominated by dizziness. The drinks were starting to have an effect. He had a low tolerance, it seemed, so he decided to slow down to avoid stumbling on the sidewalk.

As he went on his way, his wobble became more stable, but his legs still felt like they were made of rubber. His vision gradually cleared up, and the fog that flooded his mind faded.

He thrust his hands into the pockets of his jacket. With each exhalation, a small cloud blew out of his nose. He looked up at the starry night. Kevin couldn't wait to get home to hug his sister, kiss her on the forehead as he wished her good night and then throw himself at the comfort of his bed. Although, if what he'd heard about alcohol was true, then he would regret it the next morning.

Flies flew in circles around the bulb of the streetlamp over him, hypnotized, until it began to blink, turning on and off sporadically as if someone were hiding in a corner playing with the switch. The next streetlamp did the same. He wondered who stopped paying the electric bill and chuckled at his own joke, aware of how bad it was. It was the best he could do to try and calm himself.

A third lantern went out as he approached, and Kevin's smile faded.

He glanced over his shoulder and felt a shiver as he saw the streets behind him wrapped in darkness as if everything had been engulfed by a black hole. He quickened his pace. He had no reason to be afraid of the dark, that's what his parents used to tell him when he was little.

There hadn't been anything lurking in it since mankind built the concrete jungle. However…

The light of each lamp he crossed died suddenly. He walked faster. The branches of the trees collided and creaked in harmony, which didn't help to calm his nerves. He kept walking until he felt the weight of a glare on him. Kevin took a quick look around, but didn't see anyone.

His walk turned into a trot, and the trot into a sprint. The bulbs went out as he passed beneath them. The faster he ran, the more lights died.

Finally, he glimpsed the porch of his house in the distance. Kevin ran faster, his heart about to burst out from his chest, desperate to reach the door handle before being swallowed by darkness. His fingers trembled as they tried to find the key in his pockets. He finally found the right one, opened the door and dove into his house without looking back.

Everything was completely black. He could see nothing beyond his own nose. His hand groped the wall, looking for the switch. As he flipped it, the bulb exploded in a blinding glow. Sparks, and pieces of glass rained all over.

"Shit!" Kevin yelled.

He raised both hands palming the air around him. He reached the wall to his right and followed its path, using his memory to guide him up the stairs to the bedrooms.

"Dad? Jenny!"

He staggered, raising his knees more than usual to avoid tripping over the invisible steps. The wood squeaked with every step. He stopped short on the last step, the moon filling the corridor with silver reflections. One of the doors of the hallway was gnashing in the wind, wide open. It was Jenny's room.

Fearing the worst, he rushed to his sister's bedroom and stood frozen in the doorway. It took his eyes a couple of seconds to get accustomed to the darkness. But once he finally began to distinguish the silhouettes of the objects, he noticed that the place was a complete mess: the drawings were scattered on the carpet, the bed broken in half with the mattress protruded from one side as if it were overflowing water, what was once the desk had been reduced to a bunch of wooden pieces. Where was Jenny? Was she hurt? He thought of the man in black and clenched his fists until his nails dug into the palms of his hands.

For some reason he would never understand, he felt compelled to look at the ceiling. What he saw left him paralyzed. A humanoid figure hung from it on four legs. It was about seven feet tall, with two bright yellow eyes looking back at him from the gloom. It looked like a cross between a man and a skinned dog, its fingers ended in sharp claws.

Kevin felt as if the floor had crumbled beneath him. He wanted to run, but his body didn't respond. That image would haunt him for the rest of his life.

The deformed creature dropped from the ceiling, onto its four legs and approached him with the grace of a cat. Kevin held his breath, his legs trembling, his brain screaming for him to run away as far as possible. Cold sweat slipped between his fingers. Kevin stepped aside to let the beast pass, the monster's empty gaze fixed on Kevin.

Once the monster crossed the threshold into the corridor, Kevin was able to breathe again. However, the weight of the situation fell on his shoulders. He glanced around, expecting to find his sister's mutilated body covered in blood but, fortunately, he didn't see it. Jenny wasn't there.

Driven by what little judgment he had left, he hurried off into the corridor. Once outside the room, he was throw across the hallway, only saving himself from falling down the stairs by grabbing the railing with one hand. A sharp pain pierced his torso.

The clatter of crystal exploding into a thousand pieces assaulted his ears. The window at the end of the corridor was ripped out of its frame, leaving a hole like a void into the night.

Kevin jumped to his feet.

"No!"

He staggered towards the hole. All he could see was a desolate street.

Early Winter

CHAPTER 12

Patrol lights lit up the neighborhood in red and blue trails. Entire families interrupted their precious hours of sleep to witness the commotion, dressed only in gowns and pajamas. Some surrounded the yellow ribbons the police had hung around Kevin's house, others ventured into their gardens and stood on tiptoes as if an invisible wall prevented them from advancing, and a few were limited to running to their windows and watching from the comfort of their rooms. Everyone was eager to satiate some sort of morbid curiosity.

Kevin felt disgusted by them. They were just pathetic people whose lives were so boring and monotonous that they were drawn like flies to a bulb at any event, hoping to see a corpse or an arrest. They were all fucking sick. If they were in the same situation, then surely they wouldn't want a thousand eyes on them at their most vulnerable moment. They expected something exciting to happen, but the only thing on the scene was Kevin, two squad cars parked in front of his house, a couple of officers inspecting the surroundings, another two inside the house and one in front of him, holding a notebook and a pen.

"Tell me, from the beginning, everything that happened," said the officer. He touched the tip of the pen with his tongue and pressed it to the paper, prepared to write.

"I-I got home, and there was nobody in the house. All the lights were off, even the ones on the street."

"The ones outside were off?"

"Yes."

"There are some on this same street that seems to have had a short circuit." The policeman pointed over his shoulder toward the streetlamps that were still flickering.

"Inside my house was like that too," said Kevin. "When I tried to turn on the light, the bulb exploded."

"Surely, the electrical fault affected your house." The cop shrugged, and then glanced back at the notebook. "Please, continue."

"I doubt it," said Kevin. "It didn't feel that way. It was more like someone was turning them off on purpose." The officer raised an eyebrow. "I know how it sounds, but if you had been there at the time, you would know what I'm talking about."

"Please, continue," the officer repeated.

Kevin had to restrain himself from insulting him. "I went up the stairs to the second floor. I saw that my sister's room door was open, I decided to investigate and…" His throat tightened; the words refused to come out of his lips.

"Come on, boy, tell me what you know. The more you tell us, the more we'll be able to understand what happened and the more likely we'll find your sister."

"Finally," Kevin continued, "I went into my sister's room. The place was destroyed, and I saw it—a man, I think, but he didn't look like a person."

"What do you mean?" the officer asked.

"I'm not sure."

"Could you see the kidnapper's face?"

"Uh, no. I mean, yes, but…" Kevin took a breath; there was no way to put what he had just witnessed into words. "He was tall, very tall, his skin was hard as leather as if his whole body were a great scar, his claws…"

"Claws?"

"Yes, I mean, that thing, it wasn't human, I'm sure of it, but it didn't look like any animal either." Kevin hated to hear his own words; he sounded insane.

A black car stopped just in front of the house. The windows were so dark it was impossible to tell what was inside, except for the flashing lights on the windshield. A covert patrol, two men, dressed in suits got out. One wore a black suit and had a beard that apparently hadn't been groomed for weeks. His tension showed in the bags under his eyes and the gray lines in his hair. The other man was dressed in a gray suit without a single wrinkle. He looked ten years younger than his counterpart, but his manner of walking, shoulders back and head held high, gave him an air of superiority. The two were heading straight for Kevin. The bearded man rested his hand on the policeman's shoulder.

"Thank you, Officer. We'll take it from here," he said with a wink. His attention turned to Kevin. "I'm Lieutenant Spencer Cleyton, and this is FBI Agent Norman James, and we'd love to hear every little detail of what you saw tonight."

"W-well, uh, my name is Kevin Miller." His voice seemed to break with every word. "I was—I'd just arrived from a party."

"Did you drink?" Cleyton asked.

"Cleyton," James warned.

"I just want to make sure we're talking to a good witness," Cleyton said with a shrug.

"He is a good witness," said James.

"Yes, I did," admitted Kevin. "But they were just a couple of drinks, by the time I got home, I was completely sober."

"What exactly happened once you got home?" James asked.

"I went to look for my sister, Jenny," Kevin replied. "I had the feeling that something happened to her. By the time I arrived, it was too late."

"When you called nine-one-one, you mentioned seeing the kidnapper, didn't you?" asked Cleyton.

"Yes," Kevin replied hesitantly.

"Kevin," James started, "you would help us a lot if you gave us as many details as you can. I know that you're probably very shocked at the moment, so how about we go to the station, and we'll give you something to eat. You'll be able to relax and process what you just saw. We'll talk when you're ready."

Kevin hesitated for a long moment. "I saw a monster," he said at last.

James and Cleyton exchanged glances.

"I think it's better—" Cleyton began.

"I know how it sounds," Kevin interrupted. "But I'm sure of what I saw, and it wasn't human or an animal, at least not like any I've ever seen or even heard of."

"Okay, Kevin," said James. "For now, let's go to the station to get more details, okay?"

Kevin nodded reluctantly. No amount of detail was going to make him sound less crazy. Even if he showed them some evidence, they would still think what suited them. The lieutenant put a hand on the boy's shoulder and pointed to the black car in which they had arrived. Agent James reassured him with a nod as if he could sense his uneasiness. Kevin obeyed and walked, one on each side as if he were being escorted.

Kevin couldn't help turning over his shoulder to take a last look at his house, faintly hoping that Jenny would be peeking out of one of the windows or that she would come out holding hands with one of the policemen, but his prayers remained unanswered. Instead, he saw his father talking to one of the officers, obviously confused, his face contorted into a grimace with tears sliding down his cheeks. A flame set ablaze inside Kevin, a blind fury that ran through his veins. He walked towards John in big strides. He put both hands on his father's chest and shoved him to the ground.

"Where the fuck were you?" Kevin yelled. "Getting drunk in some fucking bar! You were supposed to be there with her! You were supposed to take care of her!"

A cop grabbed Kevin by the arm.

"Kev, let me explain, please," John begged, trying to get up.

"She didn't deserve this!" Kevin escaped the cop's grip, but he stood still. "You have no excuse for this. You brought us to this miserable town, and you don't even have the balls to take care of your own children."

"Come on, Kevin," said James, his voice soft as the breeze. "There's nothing more to say for now."

Kevin glared at the agent and returned his attention to the pathetic sack of meat he called Dad.

"It should've been you," Kevin said. He turned around and went on his own to the black car.

John managed to stand up and just watched Kevin being escorted away. In only one night, he had lost both of his children.

The minutes became hours, and the hours seemed like days. Being locked in an interrogation room for so long was exasperating. Kevin didn't know how there were criminals who could resist being in such a place with a straight face. The coffee steam danced freely on the table. He hadn't touched the cup since his first sip. His ribs still screamed in pain thanks to the hit he'd taken from the monster.

James looked at his watch and settled in his chair, right in front of the boy, resting his elbows on the table. He hadn't looked away from Kevin since they'd arrived. Cleyton watched from a corner, leaning against the wall with his arms folded, every now and then grunting to let them know that his patience was running out. Kevin had been repeating the same story over and over again.

"I don't know what else you want me to say," he said, staring at the table. "I already told you everything."

"Yeah, yeah, the damn giant dog climbing the ceiling," Cleyton said.

"It wasn't a dog," Kevin replied.

"So what the hell was it supposed to be? A fucking malnourished bear going from house to house kidnapping kids and jumping through windows?"

"Lieutenant," James warned.

"What?" shouted Cleyton. "Don't tell me you believe what this kid says!"

"You should," said Kevin. "Because this *kid* is the first and only witness to a kidnapping in this goddamn town."

"How are you so sure you're the only one to have seen anything?" Cleyton asked, his eyes bloodshot from exhaustion, his tongue sliding over his lips.

"You're not fooling anyone, Lieutenant," Kevin said. "Everyone knows you have nothing, even me, and I've only been living here for a couple of weeks. Besides, you saw the second floor's window. It was destroyed. You're not going to fuck around with me by saying that there is a man out there with such strength."

"You have a good point, Kevin," said James serenely. "You sound sincere, but your story doesn't make much sense. I mean, what kind of animal could get into a house and kidnap someone? If there's something I'm certain about, it's that this isn't an animal."

"I don't think it was an animal either," said Kevin.

"If it wasn't an animal," said Cleyton, "and it wasn't a person either, then I don't know what the fuck you want us to think."

"Listen, Kevin," said James, ignoring the lieutenant. "For now, I have no reason to believe you're lying. Maybe alcohol or some other substance you've consumed has distorted what—"

"I didn't consume anything," Kevin interrupted. "I mean, I did drink a little, but getting drunk doesn't make you hallucinate something like that. You can do all the tests you want. You want me to piss in a jar to prove I'm not stoned? I'll do it."

"I don't think that's necessary," said James.

"If he's up for it, I don't see why not," said Cleyton.

"I think we've had enough for today." James sighed, standing up. "Kevin, you should spend the night at a hotel with your father while they inspect your house. You two deserve to rest."

"You treat me like a nutcase!" Kevin shouted, punching the table. "I know what I say is hard to believe—"

"That's one way of putting it," Cleyton said.

"But you're not going to get anywhere by looking in the wrong place. You're just going to go in circles," Kevin said. Cleyton folded his arms and James leaned back in his chair, both of them with nothing to say. "If you can't do your job, then I'll do it myself."

Kevin jumped out of his chair and left, slamming the door behind him. Cleyton and James exchanged glances as if blaming each other.

"Little brat," Cleyton said.

"There are some things we can look into about his story," James said.

"What the fuck are you talking about? All that was a bunch of bullshit."

"Maybe not all of it."

"So you do believe that some boogeyman kidnapped his sister."

"No, but the light bulbs in his street did explode as he described, his house also suffered a short circuit, his window—"

"Whoever kidnapped the girl can break a window."

"And break the frame with sheer brute force?" James shook his head. "There's something else we are not seeing."

"Please." Cleyton sighed, waving his hand over his incipient baldness.

"We can start by investigating electrical faults. If the abductor is able to interrupt or manipulate the electric current around it, that would explain certain things."

"And how the hell would he do that?"

"Maybe he has some device that emits an electromagnetic pulse that would interfere with all the electronics around him. However, that doesn't fit with what the boy told us. I need to look into it more."

James threw back his chair, got to his feet, adjusted the buttons of his suit, and set out.

When he put his hand on the door handle, Cleyton grumbled, "You're wasting your time, Agent."

"Maybe, or maybe not. It makes sense if you think about it. It would explain how no one else has seen anything: they couldn't because it was too dark. Most disappearances have occurred at night or just after sunset, so it doesn't seem so crazy."

"We'll see who ends up being right."

"This is not a competition, Lieutenant. Innocent lives are at stake."

CHAPTER 13

The mist gently wrapped the streets in a cold embrace. Sofia's jaw rested on her hand, her distracted gaze fixed on the window, submerged in her own thoughts. The classroom was almost empty. The few students who attended were chatting as the professor arrived. They were agitated, the same way they were when a popular girl cheated on her boyfriend or one of the teachers slept with a student. That kind of gossip did not interest Sofia in the slightest. The empty words of her classmates went in one ear and out the other. However, this time they spoke louder than usual, making it hard to ignore them. She figured that whoever they were talking about had skipped class.

"No way!" cried one of the girls by her side. "The same day of the party? How awful! Poor guy must feel so guilty."

"Why would he feel guilty?"

"Because he could've been in the house taking care of her, but instead he went to the party."

"There was no way he knew that was going to happen."

"I know, but he must feel guilty anyway."

"Yeah, I guess you're right. Poor boy. I'd hate to be in his position."

Those last words sounded very familiar to Sofia, touching an open wound. Those were the kind of things they used to say behind her back when her brother disappeared. She turned to take a better look at the girls. One of them was Jessica.

As if feeling the weight of her gaze, Jessica turned to Sofia.

"Did... did you hear?" Jessica asked, seeming to try and pick her words carefully.

"No, I have no idea what you are talking about," Sofia whispered. It was the first time in a long while that she heard her own voice.

"Kevin, the new student. His sister was kidnapped yesterday right in front of his eyes."

Sofia's eyes widened. "Right in front of his eyes? Did he see who it was?"

"I'm not sure."

"What do you mean you're not sure?" Sofia's heart started racing. She had to know more.

"No one knows much." Jessica shrugged. "On Saturday night there was a party with the boys at Dave's house. Kevin went, but he had to leave early because he was worried about leaving his sister alone with his dad. I didn't understand why he acted that way, but now I know."

"His dad deserves a father of the year award," said the girl next to her.

Jessica continued as if she hadn't heard. "My mom is friends with a couple that lives on the same street. They say they heard some noises coming from the house. They looked out the window, but they didn't see anything out of the ordinary. Soon after the police came and Kevin was there talking to them. They were interrogating him because he saw everything."

Sofia couldn't believe her ears. If that guy had actually seen something, perhaps he was the key to finding her brother, or at least the bastard who had kidnapped him.

"Where is he now?" Sofia asked anxiously.

"I don't know. Not at his house, obviously, the police are still inspecting it."

"Does anyone else know?"

"The police."

Sofia pondered this for a moment. She didn't know Kevin, she didn't know anything about him. She had no way of contacting him or any idea where he might be. Or maybe she did. After all, they had something in common, and that could be enough to find him.

The clock didn't move fast enough. She felt trapped in a kind of limbo in which time had stopped. The teacher held classes normally, even though there were just a handful of people in the classroom, which annoyed her even more. Most of her classmates skipped class because they knew what happened to Kevin. After all this time of uncertainty, in which more than twenty people had disappeared, people were finally becoming aware. They were starting to fear for their lives; yet, the teacher, and the school for that matter, had decided to continue the classes as if everything were perfect. It was disgusting. Sofia thanked with all her heart the ring of the bell. She packed her things as fast as she could and left.

The white sky seemed to touch the ground. The mist didn't allow her to see beyond a few feet, but she knew the way to the park very well. Sofia crossed her arms in a poor attempt to stay warm. If she had known the weather would be like this, she would have put on a jacket, but had the weather reporter not said it would be sunny today? She shook that thought out of her mind. For some reason, it seemed disturbing. She hurried on. The sooner she could talk to Kevin, the sooner she could return home.

She reached the park and crossed the street. The scraping sound of the swings was mesmerizing. As she had thought, the place was almost deserted except for a few families that had taken their children after school. A girl screamed with joy as she slid down the slide, landed on her butt and prompted her friend to come up again. Her conversation was overshadowed by the commotion of other the children playing in the park, all of them with smiles on their faces. Their parents simply observed them sitting on benches or playing with them from time to time.

Rudy would have loved to be there. A tear slipped down her cheek, and she wiped it away. In one corner of the park, a young man sat on the ground, leaning against an oak tree, his gaze lost in the void as if he were asleep with his eyes open. Sofia gnawed her lip and walked over to him.

"You didn't go to class this morning," Sofia said.

Kevin jumped. "Son of a——" When he saw the girl, he ran his hand over his face. "Jesus. You scared the hell outta me."

"Sorry, I just wanted to talk to you for a while." Sofia sat down on the grass next to him.

"Why?" Kevin asked, frowning. "You don't even know me, I don't think we've ever even said 'hi' to each other."

"I don't know. I just thought that, maybe, it would do you good to have somebody to talk to."

"I'm fine, thanks. I've been talking to the police all night," he said with a sigh.

"I mean, with someone who understands what you are going through," she clarified.

"You don't know what——" Kevin stopped. If there were someone that who how he felt, it was she. "Everyone knows?"

"Yes. It's a small town, the news flew around. That's how it was with me."

"Look, I know you're trying to help me, but nothing you say will make me feel better. I don't want to sound like an asshole, but all I want right now is to be left alone, okay?"

"I understand."

"Thank you," Kevin said and leaned back against the oak again. Sofia also settled in. "You're not leaving."

"I know," said Sofia. "And you're right, by the way."

"About what?"

"Talking. Venting our sorrows with each other won't lead us anywhere."

"I feel like you're going somewhere with this."

"You see, the real reason I decided to talk to you was because," she paused and Kevin gestured for her to continue, "I know you saw someone."

"I didn't." Kevin shrugged.

Sofia gasped. "But—"

"But?"

"I heard you were there."

"Whatever you've heard, don't believe it." Kevin put his hand on the ground and pushed himself up. "If you'll excuse me, I'll find a place where I can be more comfortable."

"No!" Sofia cried. Kevin looked at her, confused. "I mean, you can't."

"Of course I can and I will," Kevin said and turned around, ready to leave.

"I know something. About those missing people, well, about my brother, at least, and it could be important."

Kevin slowly turned around, still standing in the same spot. "What is it?"

"I'll tell you if you tell me what you know."

"You won't believe me anyway."

Sofia let out a snort of frustration. "You're not going to give in, are you?"

Kevin shook his head. "I've had enough with the police clowns."

"Then I'll show you, but on the condition that you'll tell me what you saw."

"Done deal."

The girl sprang to her feet and brushed the dirt off her pants. "Come with me."

"Where?"

"Shut up and follow me."

Sofia led him to the east of the town until they reached a fancy neighborhood. The houses were so large they were practically mansions. The gardens and topiaries were pruned to perfection.

"I doubt the people here mow their own lawns," said Kevin.

"My parents do," she said with a faint smile. "Not that much anymore, though."

"My dad doesn't, and we're poor."

They reached a house at the end of a blind street, not as big as the others, but it seemed to be worth much more. Its walls so white they looked like pearls. Kevin glanced around and felt a knot in his stomach as he realized the neighborhood was surrounded by trees. He gathered enough courage to ask:

"A-are we near the forest?"

"You have a good eye. This entire neighborhood is on the edge of Heaven's Peak, most of the backyards go directly into the woods, including mine."

"So, this is your house."

"Well done, Sherlock, but don't get any ideas."

This time it was Kevin who smiled involuntarily. They walked around the house, and Kevin noticed that the lawn was sloppy. He remembered what she had told him about her parents and decided not to comment on it. The backyard could well be a park if given a proper treatment; it was huge, with swings and a brightly colored slide. Trees surrounded the yard and split into a path that led deep into the woods. Kevin swallowed. Sofia turned and, as if reading his thoughts, said:

"Don't worry."

With Sofia in the lead, they made their way across the path. The fog had dissipated enough they could see from a distance, but it was still there. The sky turned orange, matching with the foliage around them. The leaves on the ground crunched under their feet with every step. The noise made Kevin feel uncomfortable, vulnerable as if every leaf he crushed threatened to reveal his location to some psychopath hidden in the bushes. Sofia stopped in a clearing and shook her head.

"You know where you're going, right?" Kevin asked with a forced smile.

"Of course I know," she said, her eyes wandering.

He didn't believe her. "If this is your idea of a romantic date, then I think it's best if we stayed friends."

"This is where my brother used to play."

"Oh." Kevin did not expect that. "I'm sorry."

"There was one of us with him, always."

"So what happened?"

"I lost him." Sofia's voice cracked and she blinked back the tears. "I got distracted. I lost sight of him for just a second, and that was enough to ruin my whole family's lives."

"It's not your fault."

"Yes, it is. But, maybe, I can still do something about it."

"What do you mean?"

Sofia sighed deeply, her damp, bloodshot eyes fixed on the sunset.

"When the police came to question me, I told them that Rudy had gone to play in the woods and that was the last time I saw him. But, actually, the last thing I heard were his screams, and they came from here. But I think, no, I'm sure they didn't investigate here. I've been wanting to come for some time. I asked my sister, but she refused."

"That's why you brought me," Kevin said. He couldn't believe how naïve he had been. "You brought me here because of a hunch. This turns out to be your great secret? The small suspicion that the police didn't do something that they're basically bound to do?"

"Kevin, listen to me, if I'm right, this could be huge."

"What're you talking about?"

"I've been thinking. Maybe there's some clue, a hint of where the person who kidnapped Rudy and your sister might have gone."

Kevin turned around, ready to leave, but he stopped, an idea brewing in his mind: hope, a small chance he couldn't let escape. He knew that if he left, he would have an itch in his brain, a little voice reminding him over and over that he should have investigated the possibility a little more before dismissing it.

"Are you sure the scream came from here?" he finally asked.

"Not at all," she replied. "It was dark, and my first instinct was to go back to the house and call for help."

"But do you remember which direction it came from?"

"No, I don't think so."

"You don't think?" Kevin was starting to lose patience. He approached the girl and grabbed her by the shoulders; she didn't move. Her eyes were wide and expectant. "Close your eyes, close your eyes and remember that day, as vividly as you can." Sofia shook her head. She was about to burst into tears again. "Control yourself. You have to take control of your emotions. Don't let them take control of you."

"I don't want to go through that again."

"If you want to find Rudy, you're gonna have to."

Sofia nodded at last. She closed her eyes, and a couple of tears slid down her cheeks.

"What do you see?" Kevin asked in a whisper.

"Darkness, the woods, I can barely see the silhouettes of trees..."

"Where is Rudy?"

"I don't know," Sofia whispered. "I'm calling him, over and over again, but he doesn't answer me. I have to go back." The girl's chest started moving up and down, her breathing ragged. She was hyperventilating.

"Chill, relax, it's just a memory, okay? Take a deep breath," Kevin said. His hands went up to her face and gently caressed her cheeks. "Everything's going to be okay."

"Okay, okay," said Sofia, her eyes still closed.

She took several deep breaths until her muscles relaxed. Kevin barely noticed that she had grabbed his arms and was digging her nails into his skin, hard enough to leave red marks.

"Keep remembering," he said.

"I ran, as fast as I could, back to the house. God, it was so dark, I don't know how I found the way back. When I finally saw the windows of my house, I heard it." Sofia shuddered and opened her eyes.

"Where did the scream come from?" Kevin asked. He dropped his hands and took a few steps back.

"From over there," she said, pointing north.

"Then there we go."

Kevin slipped both hands into his jacket and started walking in the direction Sofia had pointed out. He saw over his shoulder that she was still standing in the same spot and stopped.

"Sofia, I know exactly how you feel."

"I know but—"

"But nothing," Kevin said. He moved closer to her, opened his arms and squeezed her hard.

Sofia let out a surprised sigh, shaking. After a few seconds, she settled her head on Kevin's chest and returned the hug.

Without realizing it, they were both sobbing as the sun disappeared behind them and the sky was painted purple. The crickets began their song; the night was coming to life. Kevin pulled away from her, and they both dried their tears. They stayed like that for what seemed an eternity, buried in each other's gaze. Finally, it was Kevin who broke the silence.

"Do you think they're still alive?"

"I have hope."

"If the police can't find them, we'll do it." He nodded and told her to start the search.

With nothing more to say, Sofia obeyed. As they walked, she held onto Kevin's elbow as if she couldn't stand on her own. That amused him.

"You still haven't told me what you know," Sofia said.

"I know that I know nothing."

"If you are going to quote Socrates, at least give him some credit."

"Nerd."

"I'm not joking," she said firmly. "I fulfilled my part of the bargain."

"You won't believe me. I'm sure you'll think I'm crazy or doing drugs."

She stood in front of him, folded her arms and gave him a murderous look. "Tell me."

Kevin's gaze shifted to the side, avoiding Sofia's. In the trunk of an oak, there was a mark that caught his attention. His mouth opened without a word. He wasn't sure whether to look closer or run.

"I'm waiting," Sofia insisted.

"Keep on waiting."

He put a hand on her shoulder and gently pushed her aside. He approached cautiously and narrowed his eyes. The marks were four diagonal stripes, deep scratches in the wood. Sofia followed and stood behind him, poking her head over his shoulder.

"What did that? A bear?" she asked, her voice trembling.

"They don't look like bear marks." He raised his fingers and touched it gently.

"If they are not a bear's, then what could have done that?"

Kevin turned to her; he could feel the blood leave his face. "We have to get outta here."

"What?" she asked. Kevin stepped past her, and she grabbed him by the arm. "Tell me what's going on."

"I'll tell you when we get back."

"Please don't leave me hanging," she begged.

"I know what made those marks."

He grabbed her wrist. If he had to drag her all the way back, he would. He didn't want to hurt her, but she was having a hard time keeping up with him, so he was forced to pull her on a couple of occasions. His head was spinning around them, looking everywhere. Sofia looked at him with nervous eyes. From time to time, he would ask Sofia if they were on the right path. The whole damn forest seemed exactly the same, it felt like they were trapped in a prison of trees.

Sofia stumbled over something, let out a shriek and grabbed Kevin's jacket to keep from falling. Kevin felt like his heart was about to burst from his chest, as if the slightest noise could catch the attention of whatever was lurking around.

The girl stared at the ground. There was a metallic device at her feet. She bent over, picked it up and inspected it closely. Her mouth hung open, and her eyes widened, seeming to almost slip out of their sockets.

"This is Rudy's walkie-talkie," she said at last.

The device let out a roar, a loud static that echoed in the forest. Kevin snatched it from Sofia's hands and tucked it into his jacket to silence it.

"Let's go," Kevin said.

The duo made their way back. The trees around them became shadows. In the distance, they saw the neighborhood lights and ran towards them.

Kevin let out a sigh of relief as they reached Sofia's courtyard. He had failed to notice that he was squeezing her arm a bit too firmly. He released her gently and apologized. She merely gave him a timid smile. They went around the house and agreed to see each other again soon to talk about what they had found. It was time for Kevin to tell her the truth.

CHAPTER 14

The door squealed as it opened. Particles of dust danced in columns of light that filtered through the slats of the blinds. Rob Jensen closed the door quietly behind him. The TV was turned off, and the silence was such that he could hear a buzzing in his ears. Something was wrong.

Jack's car was parked outside. The smell of freshly cooked chicken impregnated the house, yet no one was around as if his parents had vanished into thin air. He leaned into the dining room, and two plates full of food sat on the table, steam rising from them. He felt relieved. If he were lucky, he could grab a change of clothes and some money from his mom's purse and get out without being seen.

He climbed the stairs and examined the guest room and his parents' room. There was nobody in the house. He went to his room, grabbed his backpack and began stuffing it with as much clothing as he could. Then, he went into the main bedroom and moved the bedside table aside to reveal a hole in the wall, his mother's favorite place to store cash. He shoved two full stacks in his bag, put the table back in its place and prepared to leave.

In the distance, some very familiar cries caught his attention. Rob, with his heart pounding in his throat, peered cautiously out the window to find the source of the screaming.

Barely visible in the dense fog, he saw his father in the backyard with his fist wrapped around Margery's hair. He threw her to the ground next to a pool of vomit. His father's shirt was stained, so the vomit had to be his.

"Next time you put that shit on my food, I'll fucking kill you!" Jack yelled as he grabbed his wife's hair again and dragged her back to the house.

Rob went downstairs to the dining room. The kitchen door opened with a crash that shook the windows. Jack threw Margery into the table like a rag doll. Rob stood in the doorframe, not knowing how to act. Jack grabbed his plate and threw it at his wife's head; she let out a squeal.

"You'll see!" Jack shouted. "One day, you and that little shit you gave birth to are going to make me lose my patience, and you'll see my bad side! And you better pray for that day to never come because otherwise…" He froze as soon as he saw Rob. "You, you still have the balls to show your face here after what you did."

Rob's heart pounded faster, and a blind fury seized him. It was a fire that ran through his body, more and more intensely as his father approached. For a second, an image, clear as life itself, jumped into his mind. It was a man in black, his face covered by a mask, walking towards him, just as his father did at that moment.

Jack threw a swing that hit Rob's cheek. The impact forced his head to the side, but Rob did not feel any pain. His father continued by kicking him in the stomach. The air escaped Rob's diaphragm. He put both hands on his abdomen but, again, no pain. A smile flickered on the boy's face.

"What are you laughing about, you fucker?" Jack asked, his face so red that he seemed about to explode, big beads of sweat slipping down his forehead.

Rob regained his composure. He fixed his gaze on that of his father, whose eyes were bloodshot. Rob threw a punch that landed on Jack's jaw. Several teeth flew in different directions trailing blood. Rob watched with satisfaction as his father fell to his knees screaming, both hands held up to his mouth.

Margery used a chair to pull herself to her feet; her face paled and her mouth opened wide as if to scream, but the only thing that came out was the faint whine of a puppy.

"The day came, Dad," Rob said. "I lost my patience, and now you'll see my bad side."

Jack looked up with a mixture of fury and bewilderment in his eyes. He got up and threw himself at Rob with all his weight. They both crashed to the ground. Margery drowned a cry of surprise with her hands. On another occasion, the considerable weight of his father would have broken a couple of Rob's ribs, but now it was just a bother. With a grunt, Rob pushed Jack off him like a sack of potatoes.

"You son of a bitch," Jack cursed as they both stood up.

"Are you gonna let him call you that?" Rob asked his mother, who stared at him in horror.

Jack took off his belt, which unfolded to the carpet like a black snake about to attack. With the buckle in the front, Jack whipped the air, aiming directly at Rob's face. He backed away instinctively; the metal crashed against his skin and bounced off without a scratch.

A mosquito bite, Rob thought.

Jack tried to flog him again, but Rob grabbed him by the wrist and squeezed as hard as he could. He felt the bone being crushed like a soda can, and the belt slipped from Jack's hand. The cracking of bones, accompanied by his father's cries of pain, were the most satisfying things Rob had ever heard in his life.

"Stop!" Jack cried in agony. "Please!

Rob obeyed and released him as he grinned from ear to ear. Jack's hand hung from his arm, supported only by the skin, and swaying as if it were rubber. His father's eyes were redder than ever.

"H-how…" Jack stammered.

Rob opened his mouth to answer but was interrupted by a shriek behind him. He turned around. His mother was trembling, whiter than ever, holding a butcher's knife in both hands as if it were a bat. She jumped towards Rob with frantic eyes. Rob tried to dodge her, but the blade dug into his chest, right in the heart. Margery pushed the knife as best she could before releasing it.

A sharp pain pierced his chest. It was unreal to see that long piece of metal buried in him. He put both hands on the handle and pulled it out with a grunt. Only the tip of the knife was red, barely an inch.

"How…how dare you?" Rob asked his mother. "After all the shit this monster has done to you, you decide to defend him?"

Jack crawled to the stairs like a startled worm. Rob dropped the knife and grabbed Margery by the throat. He lifted her above him as she kicked and buried her nails in his hand in a vain attempt to free herself. He squeezed harder and made the bone at the back of her neck detach from the spine.

Crack.

He threw his mother's body to the ground. The woman fell belly down, her head contorted back over her shoulder, her eyes staring at the ceiling with a look of astonishment. Rob hoped to feel relieved, perhaps guilty, but he felt nothing. Maybe because even though his mother was also a victim during most of her marriage, that did not redeem the fact that she had let Jack do whatever he wanted with little Rob.

He picked up the knife and walked cautiously up the stairs. He didn't want his prey to know he was coming. Rob barely noticed that he was smiling, amused at the thought that he was playing cat and mouse.

Rob opened the door to his room. Everything looked the same. There was only a mattress where the bed was supposed to be, the same one he broke while jumping on it as a child. His father gave him a horrible beating that day, and he still had the scars to show it. Jack had yelled that Rob would sleep on the floor since then, and he did.

Rob looked around. Nothing else to see. The closet was too small for that ball of fat to fit in, so he dismissed it as a hiding place.

He entered the guest room and stood right in the middle. He put one knee on the floor and inspected under the bed. Nothing. He went to the closet and opened it wide, only clothes. He went into the bathroom and opened the shower curtain; no one. On his way back, he saw out of the corner of his eye a monstrous figure slipping past the bathroom mirror at the same time as he. He paused for a moment to make sure that what he had seen was real.

What glanced back at him wasn't his reflection, but a twisted version of himself. His face had turned white as snow, his eyes black as coal, and he could see purple veins drawn on his neck, throbbing as if they were about to explode. For some reason, the uncanny image made him laugh. All his life he had felt like a monster, and now his appearance reflected it. His white sweater had black spots down his neck and shoulders. Again, he could see a masked man, this time behind him, whispering in his ear.

With the knife in hand and a smile on his face, Rob went straight to the only place left for his father to hide, the main bedroom. Along the way, he began humming Led Zeppelin's "Stairway to Heaven," one of his favorite songs.

He stopped in front of the wooden door and stared at it for a second. Jack was on the other side, he could smell the blood spurting from his broken jaw. It was the man who had made Rob suffer, who had insulted and beat him since he could remember, but still, he hesitated. Perhaps, deep down, a small part of him loved his father. A tear slipped down his cheek, and he clenched his fist around the handle of the knife. He both hated him and loved him. Jack never gave him the slightest sign of affection, and on top of that, made life a living hell for him and his mother. Such an awful person didn't deserve to live.

With a kick, the door flew out of its frame, landing on the other side of the room as wood chips jumped in all directions. The next thing he felt was a blow to the right side of his head. It was so strong that it pushed him to the side, accompanied by a deafening roar that left him with a buzzing in his ear. Rob used the wall beside him to keep his balance and cursed at the top of his lungs. A piercing pain from the side of his head made him touch a circular wound and what appeared to be a small stone buried in his skin. He pulled it out with his fingernails and threw it to the ground in a fit of anger; the metallic sound it produced revealed that it was a bullet. He turned his gaze to his right, where his father sat in a corner with his eyes wide open and his good hand wielding a pistol whose mouth exhaled a wisp of smoke.

"How the fuck are you still alive?" Jack stammered, his whole body shaking like jelly. "I shot you in the head."

Rob strode toward him. Jack pulled the trigger again. The bullet hit Rob's chest, and the impact made him stagger. He nearly lost his balance again but held on. He pushed forward, ripped the gun from Jack's hand and tossed it to the side.

He put both hands on his father's head and looked straight into his eyes. Jack began to sob, his nose like a fountain of snot that mingled with the blood in his mouth, trembling so hard that Rob had to make an effort to keep him still. His father's pants revealed a stain that ran down his leg to his ankle. A pool of urine spread between his feet.

"You are pathetic," Rob said.

Rob pressed his hands to Jack's head as hard as he could. The giant's babbling became screams of pain, his eyes reddened, and his nose began to sputter blood. Rob felt the skull of his father split between his palms like a watermelon until it exploded in a crimson mixture of flesh, brains, and bone.

CHAPTER 15

Kevin woke up, sweating as if he were melting. He turned his head to the side and found John still sleeping peacefully in the bed next to him. Kevin put his head back on the pillow, staring at the ceiling. In a couple of minutes, his vision adjusted to the darkness of the hotel room. They had to spend the night there while the police investigated their house. The police had told them that it would take twenty-four hours, which meant that he could return to the comfort of his room the next day.

But that thought, instead of reassuring him, only disturbed him even more. He would be returning to the same place where Jenny was kidnapped, where he had seen the strange creature.

He pushed back the sheets and stood up, dragging his bare feet into the bathroom. He turned on the light and locked himself in. For the first time in his sixteen years, he found two black bags under his eyes. Not surprising, as he had barely managed to sleep for a couple of hours, and those hours had been filled with nightmares that, thankfully, he barely remembered. Nothing more than fleeting and blurry images that reproduced one on top of another.

Next to the sink was a small bag that his dad had managed to take before going to the hotel. Kevin opened it, reached in and found a bottle of sleeping pills. He still didn't know why his father still carried them with him, considering that alcohol put him to sleep just fine.

He stared at the bottle for a while. It shouldn't be too difficult, he just had to take a good handful, maybe take a bottle of vodka from John and down them all in a single gulp. Then everything would end, all his pain, in a blink. He would simply go to sleep and never wake up.

Kevin tried to fight those thoughts, but the idea was so tempting that he surprised himself with a handful of pills in his mouth. In a moment of sanity, he spat them out. He couldn't let himself get carried away. He couldn't be so cowardly and so pathetic, especially when his sister could still be alive, suffering, all by herself somewhere. He remembered Rudy's walkie-talkie and Sofia's expression when they found it. Not everything was lost. There was still a trace of hope.

He picked up all the pills and put them back into the bottle. He sealed it as hard as he could, then put it back in John's bag. Kevin opened the tap and poured cold water on his face. He groped blindly until he found a towel to dry his face on, which made him feel a little better.

Kevin looked up, hoping to find his own reflection returning his gaze. Instead, he saw a man dressed in a black coat, a mask the color of his skin, embedded in his face like melted leather, two empty sockets where his eyes should be. Kevin screamed and backed up until he hit the wall. His bare foot slipped on a puddle of water, causing him to fall to the ground. Trembling, he could hear the beating of his own heart, mingled with John knocking at the door.

"Kev! Are you all right, champ?" his father asked on the other side.

Kevin couldn't answer. He leaned against the sink and sat up. Now there was his own reflection in the mirror, white as paper. Kevin opened the door. His father received him on the other side, rubbing his eyes, still half asleep.

"I'm fine, Dad," said Kevin, trying to hide how much he was shaking. "I just had a bad dream, and I'm still waking up."

"Are you sleepwalking?" John asked. "You've never done it before. Well, I suppose there's a first time for everything." He approached Kevin with open arms. "Kev, I know what's been going on is hard."

"I'm fine, Dad," Kevin said, pushing his father aside. "I just need to get back into bed."

The boy stepped out of the restroom and threw himself on the soft mattress, courtesy of the hotel.

"Do you want me to turn on the TV for a while?" John asked before going to bed.

"Yeah, whatever."

John grabbed the remote control and turned on the small television. The news channel came on, bright on the screen. An attractive reporter told them what the weather would be over the next few days. She advised viewers to look for resources and prepare to take shelter in their homes the next few days because a snowstorm was coming.

"So early in the season for a blizzard," said John. "What crazy weather we got."

Kevin leaned back on his pillow, ignoring his father's comments. He didn't have much time. He had to get going as soon as possible. He had to find Jenny by the time the storm arrived, otherwise it might be too late.

CHAPTER 16

The Sanders' house was spacious. The walls, covered with floral wallpaper, displayed old pictures and family portraits. Archaic decorations and antiques rested on the shelves. A particular porcelain doll didn't seem to look away from James, who leaned forward on the couch to reach the coffee that Mrs. Sanders, a blonde woman in her fifties with bushy eyebrows, had just served.

"Thank you very much, Mrs. Sanders," said James. "You didn't have to bother."

"Of course I had to, Agent," she responded with a smile. "It's the least I can do. You spend day and night trying to catch the criminal who's terrorizing our little piece of heaven. And please call me Evelyn. For me, the word 'missus' is worse than swearing."

"Evelyn, as you know, a few days ago we took Harry into custody for suspicious behavior." Evelyn's smile disappeared as quickly as it had emerged. "Is there anything you know about this?"

"Agent, I don't know what kind of people Harry has been hanging out with, but I assure you that he's not really like those people. He's a good boy. He always has been."

"What was he like before?"

"He was raised in a Christian household. He had good grades and played sports. Just because he deviated a little from the Lord's way doesn't mean he's a lost cause. As a mother, I know my child and whatever is going on with him is temporary. He will soon realize his mistakes and follow God's teachings like he's always done."

"If Harry has always been a good kid, then what made him behave so erratically?" James asked, avoiding her eyes.

"The truth is, I have no idea. I would tell you if I knew."

"Mrs. Sanders—"

"Evelyn."

"Evelyn," James corrected, "you're telling me he's always been a good young man, so such a drastic change in behavior must have been caused by something. Are you sure you don't know what might have caused that? Were there any family issues? Or maybe he got in trouble in school?"

"No, everything's quiet at home. Since his father passed away, God has him in his glory, it's been just him and me, and we've never had any problems. Although, now that you mention it, Harry began to have night terrors recently."

"Night terrors?"

"Yes, he would wake up screaming in the middle of the night. He would have very vivid, and very graphic, nightmares that gave him panic attacks. A friend of mine has a son who had them as a child, but Harry never had them until recently."

James didn't know what to think. There seemed to be no connection between nightmares and the behavioral change, but perhaps they were the psychological effect of some drug. If so, it still wouldn't explain much.

"Interesting," he said out loud.

"Agent, may I ask, what was he doing that you had to arrest him as if he were a criminal? People are talking already, saying all sorts of nasty things. When the police came, they told me they were going to interrogate him, but I haven't heard anything else since then."

James hesitated before replying. It was probably worth telling her the full story if he wanted more information.

"We found him in an abandoned house on the outskirts of town, near Bachman Avenue."

"Doing what?" she asked.

"Wearing a mask in the middle of the night. We'd received an anonymous call that same night reporting suspicious activity in the area. We believe the place we found him in is a meeting spot for drug trafficking."

"Oh, my God." Mrs. Sanders placed her hand on her chest.

James took a sip of coffee and placed the mug on the table. He must have looked uneasy because Mrs. Sanders asked him, "Do you want me to bring you anything other than coffee?"

"No, no thanks, I'm fine."

"Don't be embarrassed, Agent, feel yourself at home. Give me a moment, and I'll make you some lemonade."

Evelyn got up, adjusted her dress, and headed for the kitchen before James could protest. He put both hands to his face and rubbed it. He couldn't wait to get out of there, he hadn't told her about Harry yet, and he wasn't going to do it until he had a clue. It was for the best. He already had experience in such situations. If he told her before, surely she would blame him or be too distressed to continue talking about the subject.

James remembered the night he had found his wife on the restroom floor, with a bottle of pills on her side. He had called an ambulance and stayed up all night by her side waiting for her to tell him that everything was going to be okay. That never happened. He was interrogated, but he barely answered a handful of questions. All he wanted was to be with her again, nothing else.

However, that wasn't the reason why he personally went to talk to Mrs. Sanders. He made that decision because of what the coroner had shown them: Harry's skull had been fractured, but not by a blunt object. It looked more like it was crushed. James couldn't even imagine how anybody would be able to do something like that.

Besides, who would do it? James first thought was that one of the officers might have sneaked into Harry's cell and killed him. However, that would make Reyes a suspect because he was the only one with access. So either the person responsible managed to sneak past him or simply had the authority to do so. That would throw the sheriff and Cleyton in there. Something didn't feel right. Could it be that Harry Sanders killed himself? No, that was impossible. How could anyone crush their own head? Perhaps a conversation with Mrs. Sanders would give James some insight.

Finally, Mrs. Sanders arrived with a glass of freshly made lemonade. James thanked her and drank half of it despite not being a fan of homemade juices.

"Where did you say you found him?" Evelyn asked.

"Near Bachman Avenue, in an abandoned house," James responded. He didn't feel comfortable sharing so much information with someone outside the investigation, but he figured there was no other choice.

"And after you arrested him, did you check inside the place?" she asked.

Of course, the agent wanted to reply; however, a shadow of doubt clouded his mind.

"I'm sure the team took care of that."

"I'm sure they did," she said with a smile.

James finished the lemonade while thinking. He had made the report about the incident, but he didn't know if somebody else had bothered to take a look around the place. He had been so focused on Sanders that it had slipped by him, and he was sure Cleyton hadn't done it. Maybe it would be for the best if James were to go by himself that same day. After all, he'd be able to have a better look in broad daylight.

"When would you say that Harry's weird behavior started?" James asked.

"A few days ago. He got home late one night, covered in mud. Well, I don't know if it was mud. Some black substance, like oil or something. I never managed to wipe the stain away. That was the first time I noticed something was wrong. Keep in mind, I'm talking about someone who not long ago asked for permission to take out the trash."

A black substance, maybe the same one he carried in his pocket. The same one he spat on Cleyton's face.

"Do you know where Harry said he would be that night?"

Evelyn shook her head, but then she stopped and looked up as if trying to remember something.

"No, although, now that I think about it, I think I've heard something about a homework assignment. About the town's history."

"Mrs. Sanders—"

"Evelyn."

"I'm sorry. Evelyn. Do you still have Harry's clothes from that day? The one with the stain?"

"Why, of course," she said, standing up and heading for the kitchen. "I didn't want to throw it out because it was a shirt his father had given to him years ago."

James waited for her to return. She was carrying a plastic bag with the shirt inside.

"Evelyn, did you touch the shirt with your hand?" James asked. Whatever that substance was, he had the feeling it was dangerous.

"Oh, God, no," said Evelyn, looking at him as if he'd accused her of some horrible crime. "It was gross, I wore gloves the whole time."

"I'm glad."

James stood up, grabbed the bag and closed it tightly. The smell made him frown.

"Evelyn, did you know the Everett family?"

Her expression changed. All of a sudden, her cheery demeanor vanished.

"I know who they are, but neither me nor my son had any contact with them."

"What about the Millers?"

"If you're implying that my son had anything to do with the kidnapping of those kids, then you're wrong!" she shouted, her face red with rage.

"I'm not implying anything. All I want is to get to the truth, and that means exploring all possible scenarios."

"Then I don't know what you're doing here. I got questioned about Harry when you dragged him to jail like a dog."

"Actually, Mrs. Sanders." James lowered his gaze. There was no easy way to say it. "I came to inform you about what happened to Harry while in custody. We found him dead yesterday night. I'm very sorry for your loss."

Evelyn's face twisted in a mix of horror and sorrow. Her trembling lips managed to form one single phrase:

"Get out of my house."

CHAPTER 17

The high school's hallways were desolate. It had been two hours since classes had ended, so it wasn't all that strange to find that the only people there were the cleaning staff and a few teachers. Kevin made his way without even looking where he was going. He already knew the way from memory. The echo of his own steps tumbled in his ears. He hated the silence. It was like death: passive, indifferent and threatening. Silence never meant anything good.

Kevin stopped in front of the wooden door to classroom 302. He didn't have the slightest idea what he was going to ask or how to broach a subject like that with a teacher. He stood on his tiptoes to look through the small window at the door. Mr. Wolf sat at his desk, hidden in a pile of papers, evaluating the student's tests.

Kevin hadn't had much hope of finding him, but now that he had, he wasn't sure if he wanted to proceed. He took a breath and entered without knowing what to expect. It could be either a dead end or the key to finding his sister.

As soon as he stepped in, he was greeted by an army of empty desks, aligned perfectly, and an obese man sitting at the teacher's desk. His gray and thick beard had properly earned him the nickname: Santa Claus.

"Excuse me, Mr. Wolf, can I bother you for a minute?"

Santa Claus looked up and took off his glasses. "You're excused. Please make yourself comfortable. I'm happy to be bothered."

"Are you sure I'm not interrupting anything?"

"No, not at all," he said, putting the pen aside. "I know most will fail the test anyway, so don't worry." Kevin let out a nervous laugh, unsure if he was joking or not. "These are from your class, by the way. Do you want to know your results?"

"Uh, no thanks." He wasn't in the mood to see his failures. The reason for his visit was completely different.

"You made the trip all the way here when there's not a single soul out, but it is not to find out your results," said Wolf, surprised. "Now you have my undivided attention."

Kevin took a seat at one of the desks. "See, Mr. Wolf, there are a couple of things I would like to know. I went to the local library this morning, but it didn't answer any of my questions. Actually, I ended up with more questions than what I started with."

"Please tell me how I can help you," Wolf said. He seemed enthusiastic. "Is it about some assignment for another class?"

"I guess you could say that," Kevin shrugged. "You know a lot about the history of this town, don't you?"

"I wouldn't be teaching otherwise. Of course, I like to think that I know a lot about history in general. Having grown up here, I can say for sure that I do have knowledge about this town particularly. You, on the other hand, are a new addition to the town."

"Yeah, the new kid on the block."

"And what do you think about it?"

"It's a little peculiar for my taste."

"Peculiar," repeated Wolf with a nod. "That's the right word, no doubt."

"I would like to know more about the history of Heaven's Peak."

"I'm afraid you should be more specific," he said, smiling slyly under his beard. "If you want me to explain the history of the town as a whole, it would serve to pay attention in my classes."

The truth was that he didn't know where to start, which might be why he hadn't had much success in the library. On the one hand, there was the vast forest that surrounded the town, which he was sure had something hidden underneath. On the other hand, there were the disappearances. After spending countless hours looking through old newspapers, he hadn't been able to find any incident related to the disappearances from the last five years. It was as if people simply ceased to exist.

"What can you tell me about the area?" Kevin asked. "I mean, out in the woods, if there is one particular place worth mentioning."

"Do you ever look out the window of your house? The whole town is surrounded by trees."

"Yeah, I mean—" Kevin sighed. "What I mean is, is there something dangerous in the woods?"

"Bears, I suppose." Mr. Wolf shrugged.

"That's not what I had in mind." Kevin leaned back in his chair. "Besides, there are not supposed to be bears in Heaven's Peak."

"Bear hunting was formerly a popular sport, but one day they simply stopped appearing. Some people say that they migrated to avoid humans, others that they simply hunted all the bears in the area. It's unlikely but possible."

"I'm sorry, sir, but I didn't come to talk about bears."

"And I still don't know what you want to talk about." Wolf opened the drawer to his right and took out a cigarette. "Does it bother you if I smoke?"

"Not at all," Kevin said, frowning. "What about the fire alarm?"

"It broke the day before yesterday, some electrical mishap if I'm not mistaken. Don't tell your classmates, Miller. This is confidential." Kevin zipped his lips with his fingers. "Anyway, what did you want to talk about?"

"About the forest," Kevin reminded him. "Well, about strange events happening in the woods."

"This is about your sister, isn't it?" he asked, leaning over the desk. A look of compassion filled his face; his breath smelled of nicotine.

"I just want answers."

"I understand. I know our local police have not produced much in the way of results, but I'm sure they're doing everything in their power to solve these crimes."

"The police? Yeah, right."

Mr. Wolf frowned in confusion. "You're not much of a fan of their work, from what I see."

"I told them what I saw," said Kevin, looking down. "I told them everything, and they discarded it, just because it wasn't what they wanted to hear."

Kevin didn't notice that he was red as an apple and his knuckles paled as he clenched his fists. The teacher puffed his cigarette before giving his opinion. "Maybe what you told them wasn't relevant to the investigation, haven't you thought about that?"

"Except that it was, and still is. They are going in the wrong direction."

Wolf opened another drawer, took out an ashtray and extinguished the cigarette in it. He leaned forward, placing his elbows on the table. "Kevin, I'll answer whatever you ask me with only one condition: promise me you won't do anything stupid. And by stupid, I mean nothing that puts your safety or that of others at risk, and you'll let the police do their job."

"I promise," Kevin lied.

"Very well."

"Now, is there a dangerous place in the forest? One of those places that tourists are warned not to go or something?"

The teacher shrugged but put a hand on his thick beard in a reflective manner.

"The closest thing I can think of is an abandoned mansion on the outskirts of Heaven's Peak. It belonged to a wealthy family more than a century ago. One of its occupants, I'm not sure if it was the father or one of his servants, went crazy one night and killed the others. He fled, and was never found."

A mansion would be the perfect hiding place for a serial killer, or at least it would be if that were the situation, but it wasn't like that, and Kevin couldn't find the connection between that incident and the creature he saw.

"Any others?"

"There are also coal mines that stopped operating almost twenty years ago. A company that saw the potential of the site in the 1950s bought the land, and over the next ten years, the economy of Heaven's Peak prospered. But then the fire of '61 happened, many people got scared and decided to close the place. There had been incidents before. The ground they were working on was unstable, and the electricity would malfunction from time to time, and that was a serious issue. I think that's why the fire occurred."

"I don't understand."

"See, coal mines contain toxic gases such as carbon dioxide and methane. Methane is a highly flammable gas, and if enough is concentrated in a closed place, a simple spark can lead to a big explosion. When the gas levels are low enough, people can work there using a ventilation system. However, if the percentage of methane is as much as five percent you run the risk of a disaster. Continuing to work there meant risking an explosion so massive it would not only kill everyone inside but force the inhabitants of Heaven's Peak to evacuate the town."

"Wow, seriously? Would the explosion be that bad?"

"The explosion itself wouldn't be. Mine explosions can also occur from coal dust particles. Normally there's not enough dust in the air for that to happen, but if a methane explosion were to occur, the blast would spread the dust in the air where the heat would ignite it, which would intensify the energy of the explosion."

"It would be like a chain reaction."

"Exactly. In 1961, a small fire near there alerted everyone. It was contained in time, but it was agreed that continuing to work there meant a risk to the population, so they decided to evacuate. Until today, no one has dared to return."

"Incredible," Kevin managed to say.

"I know, right?"

"And what about local legends? Supernatural creatures and stuff like that."

"Now we are going into the terrain of mythology," Mr. Wolf pointed out. "It is a rather abrupt leap from our previous conversation topic."

"I like that kind of stuff," Kevin lied. "Spooky stories and all that. Besides, the folklore is always related to the history of a place, right?"

"I guess you're right in that regard," he admitted. "Truth be told, I'm not sure what to tell you. It's not my specialty. I can tell you a little about the natives who lived here before the colonization."

"Yes, of course," said Kevin.

"The tribes who inhabited these mountains believed in various spirits," Wolf explained. "Their belief system was based on animism and shamanism. According to them, everything in this world has a soul, an essence, a spirit: from the trees to stars, people, animals, and even objects. However, some of these spirits had no connection to the physical realm and could take possession of a human being."

"Like demonic possession?"

"No, it's very different. Demonic possession as you and I know it comes from the Christian belief system telling us the entities that take possession of a human being are evil by nature. The spirits that these tribes referred to, however, could be benevolent or malicious. Therefore, several branches of the same religion were born, as some decided to worship one entity while condemning another."

Kevin had never been particularly interested in the supernatural, as he couldn't help but compare it with religion. People reported their experiences with miraculous or fantastic events while others just never had them, so he never paid much attention to the subject. Now, things were different. His sister's life was at risk, and he was determined to do everything possible to find her, even if he had to fall into madness, chase things out of this world, or die trying.

If he was certain of anything, it was that what he saw that night wasn't a spirit. He saw it up close. He heard its claws scratching the floor as it moved and the creaking of the wood on which it walked. The putrid smell of dead flesh was something he would never forget in his life. Unless that monster was possessed by something, but then that would mean...

"If one of those spirits possessed a human being, would it change the person?" Kevin asked. "Physically, I mean."

"I know I told you not to compare it with Christianity, but in the Christian religion, the allegedly possessed do present physical changes such as pale skin, black eyes and the body writhing in strange positions, if you believe in that kind of thing, of course. So I wouldn't be surprised if the natives also believed on physiological changes on the possessed ones. I'm sorry that my answer is so vague but, as I said, I'm not very familiar with the subject."

"If they suspected that a person was possessed by an evil spirit, how would they exorcise them?"

"It depends on the severity of the situation," Wolf replied. "If the person were possessed for a short amount of time or dominated by a weak spirit, they would perform a ritual or some ceremony to eradicate it. If the case was severe, they were said to use a 'Divine Light.'"

"That doesn't sound vague at all," Kevin said sarcastically.

"It's open to interpretation, like every reputable religion."

"Thank you so much, Mr. Wolf."

"Is there anything else I can help you with?"

While it wasn't what he expected, he had more answers than before and, most importantly, a few places to investigate. Kevin shook his head, apologized and thanked his teacher once again before leaving.

His next stop was Sofia's house. His mind quickened, thinking about everything they would need for the expedition.

CHAPTER 18

James stopped at the red light and cursed his luck. He didn't even bother going back to the station to make sure someone had returned to the abandoned house after catching Sander. He was sure no one did. Besides, even if they had, he was driven to go there anyway, as if the house were a huge magnet and he was a small piece of metal, a victim of fate.

The light turned green, and James hit the pedal with all his strength. It wouldn't take him long to get there.

His undercover car's radio came to life, although he couldn't identify which officer's voice came out of the device. There was an emergency at the intersection of King's Road, in the opposite direction of where James was heading. He was tempted to ignore the call, but his hand went straight to the radio as if it had a life of its own. He identified himself and notified them that he was on his way.

James made a U-turn, completely ignoring the traffic laws. For a call like that, it'd better be very important. It took him about five minutes to get to the site. Three squad cars were already on the scene, blocking the road. He had to park one block away and walk. He adjusted his tie and buttoned his suit as he stepped out of the car and strode to the house from which the commotion came. It was a small two-story residence with a little wear on the wood. It was humble but, apart from that, it didn't seem to stand out from the homes around it.

Several policemen went in and out of the residence. One of them ran out, trying to cover his mouth with both hands, a thread of vomit draining between his fingers. What was going on? Finally, he found a familiar face among the group of uniformed men.

"Reyes," called James, making his way through the crowd. "What's the situation?"

Reyes looked up, put his hand on James' shoulder and led him into the house.

"I'll show you."

They walked through the living room to the dining room. At the foot of the stairs, a man in a suit was crouched, taking pictures of a woman's body lying on the floor. She seemed to be in her forties, her face pale, her dead eyes looking at the ceiling, her neck contorted back like the head of an owl. James swallowed. The situation seemed obvious; however, there was something that worried him to the core of his being.

"Who is she?" asked the agent.

"Margery Jensen," Reyes replied. "Housewife, mother. Seems to have a broken neck, so it's not difficult to deduce the cause of death. Still, the coroner will give us a more concrete answer."

"I don't want to sound like a smartass but, from what I see, it looks like she fell down the stairs. I don't see the reason why everyone is so freaked out."

"That's not where the fun ends," Reyes said with a smile. He escorted James to the main bedroom on the second floor. "I introduce you to Mr. Jensen," he said, opening the door.

In the middle of the room lay a man's body. He was huge, probably six foot four and weighing around two hundred pounds. His limbs were stretched out to the sides like a human X. His head, or rather what used to be his head, was pulverized. Scattered all over the carpet in a pool of blood, mixed with white pieces of skull, were the pink bits of what was left of his brain. A tongue peeled through the clotted mass, decorated with just a few fragments of teeth.

James took a step back, put his fist to his mouth and bit his knuckles.

"Wh-what the fuck?"

"That's exactly what I said when I saw it," Reyes said. "I don't know how the fuck someone could do something like that. I can only imagine a huge hammer, the kind that they use in constructions to break cement."

"Doesn't it remind you of...?"

"The boy Sanders? Yeah, you don't have to tell me that. The difference is that we could at least tell it was Sanders. This one seems like a bomb exploded in his brain."

James took a moment to assess the situation. Something they both had in common was their shattered heads. Was there any way to apply so much pressure to someone's skull for it to be crushed like that? It wasn't something he wanted to find out, but he had to.

"Is there anybody else?" James asked.

"No, just them. Their son, Rob Jensen, is missing."

Suddenly, the memory of Harry's shirt jumped into his mind. It was still wrapped in a plastic bag in the trunk of his car.

"Did they find anything else?" James asked. "Any object, a garment or whatever, with black goo on it?"

Reyes frowned at him, confused.

"Black goo? No, not that I know of."

"Shit."

James left the room and searched everywhere in the house, inspecting the bodies closely and with enough tact to avoid compromising the scene. He examined every inch of that house without any success. However, something else caught his attention. He paused his search to ask one of the officers, "Excuse me, where is Lieutenant Cleyton?"

"I have no idea, maybe at the station. People are saying he's looking pretty bad, so I don't know if he's there or took the day off."

"What do you mean? Was he sick?"

"I don't know, Agent." The officer shrugged. "I'm just telling you what I heard."

"I have to go," James said.

Before the officer could reply, the agent was already out the door. James told Reyes he had an important issue to which he needed to attend, and if anyone asked about him to tell them that he had found something important about the case, nothing more and nothing less. Reyes nodded. James left the residence and jogged to his car.

As he drove away, he thought of going to the station first to confront Cleyton before it was too late, but no one would pay attention to James, and the idea inside his mind was so insane that even he was having trouble getting his head around it.

That black goo had something to do with all of it. Maybe it was some kind of contagious disease that made people go crazy? It was a long shot, like something out of the Twilight Zone, but something inside him, some kind of force, drove him to look into it like a moth drawn to a light bulb. He needed more evidence. A dirty t-shirt was not enough.

One more piece of the puzzle, he thought, *one more piece and it will all make sense.*

With nothing else in mind, James made his way to the abandoned house.

CHAPTER 19

⁓

Kevin knocked again. He still hadn't gotten used to how fancy Sofia's neighborhood looked. He waited a while before knocking again. Just as he raised his fist, he heard footsteps coming from the other side. They were heavy, like those of a giant who had just awakened from their sleep. He swallowed as the door opened, expecting to see Sofia's father.

To his surprise, on the other side was a blonde girl of small stature, with doll-like features and curvy eyebrows that made her look angry.

"Who are you?" asked the girl.

"Uhh, I'm Kevin, Kevin Miller, is Sofia home?"

"No," she replied.

"Let him come up!" Sofia shouted from the second floor.

"What?" the girl yelled. "I won't let you bring a boy to your room!"

From the corner at the top of the stairs, Sofia's head popped out; her hair was damp and disheveled, but still, so long it almost touched the ground. She looked beautiful.

"I'm not that kind of girl, Lia," said Sofia. "Let him in, it's important."

"How important?" Lia insisted.

"Excuse me," Kevin said, gently pushing her aside.

"Where do you think you are going?" Lia said, standing before him again, cutting him off.

"To Sofia 's room. If you don't want to listen, put on some headphones."

"Kevin!" Sofia yelled, peeping out again, this time with a relentless look.

"You and I are going to have a serious conversation," Lia said to Sofia with the severity of a mother.

"You're younger than me!" Sofia yelled.

"Exactly," Lia replied.

"Calm down, both of you," Kevin said, turning his attention to Lia. "We're going to finish a project that should've been done by now, and we have only two days left to bring it. We wouldn't be in this problem if *someone* didn't forget to do her research in advance." He looked at Sofia as if trying to blame her.

She hesitated for a second, still trying to understand what was going on. Once she figured it out, she followed suit.

"I already said I was sorry," said Sofia with puppy eyes. Kevin had to make an effort not to laugh at her acting skills.

"An apology is not going to save us from an F," he said.

"All right," Lia said, crossing her arms. "I'll keep an eye on you two."

Sofia nodded, and Kevin went upstairs. The second floor hallway reminded him of the one at his house. The image of the broken window came to mind, but he shook those thoughts away. Sofia led him to a room on her left. It was rather small, with a variety of toys arranged along several shelves, so orderly that they could be part of a plastic army. The blue wall contrasted with the small bed's red sheets; on top of the night table were some car drawings and a stereo. Despite the bright mood, Kevin felt a heavy burden on his shoulders. Sofia stood by the door.

"It's been a while since someone else has been here," she said.

"Is this your brother's room?" Kevin asked. Sofia nodded. "Where's the other walkie-talkie?"

"In one of the drawers of the night table, I don't know which one."

Kevin sat on the edge of the bed, facing the stereo, and rifled through the nightstand's drawers until he found some batteries, a flashlight and finally, buried under several cables for who knew what, the other walkie-talkie. He took the one they had found in the forest out of his jacket and compared them. They looked exactly alike, but one had been damaged by the damp earth.

"I think we have a winner," Kevin said. "Do you have a map? Of the town, I mean."

"A map? Uh, yeah, I think. There are flyers for tourists everywhere. Heaven's Peak is still a resort town."

"No, I don't mean some commercial map for the public. I need something more detailed, maybe some historical map, you know what I mean?"

"I think I do. I'll see if I can find one, why do you want it?"

"Our history teacher, Mr. Wolf, gave me an interesting idea. I went to visit him before I came here."

"Explain."

"I have a hunch," Kevin said. More than that, he was sure they were on the right track. "We're going into the woods, so we better get acquainted with the area."

Sofia raised her eyebrows so much that they seemed to disappear into her scalp. "What, are you crazy? We're going to the woods again?"

"We have to. I mean, think about it. This is a small town so there are not that many places where someone, or something, could hide. People don't just disappear, they are taken somewhere. I am sure that place is in the woods, or at least close to it."

"It does make sense." She didn't seem very happy to admit it.

"The teacher told me about two places. One is an abandoned coal mine, the other is a mansion on the outskirts of the town. I don't think the mansion has much relevance, it's not a very good hiding place, I think. And surely someone nearby would have noticed something strange. The coal mine, though, sounds like the perfect spot, but..."

"But what?"

"According to Wolf, the site was evacuated because of toxic gases, so it must be very dangerous to walk around there. Unless someone kept the ventilation system working."

"And you think that's possible?"

"Yeah, except that it only makes sense for several people to do it. You know, to do maintenance and keep anybody else from finding out about it."

Sofia crossed her arms like she was trying to hug herself as if winter had suddenly arrived. It was no wonder, after all, the blizzard would come later that same night.

"I think we should tell the police," Sofia said.

Kevin couldn't believe what he was hearing. "Why should we?"

"Because it's their job! We'll tell them we found my brother's walkie-talkie in the woods. If they have at least half a brain, they will connect the dots as we did and they'll come to the same conclusion, or we can simply tell them to investigate the mines. I mean, I don't see why we should risk ourselves."

"I can't," Kevin said, shaking his head. "I can't do that. It would be like giving up. I wouldn't be solving the problem, I would just be giving it to them to solve for me, which I know they won't do."

"Why do you think that?" Sofia asked.

"Because they haven't done so in five years. If there's the slightest possibility that I may find my sister, with or without help, I'll take it. Besides, I don't know if you heard, but a fucking blizzard is on its way to strike tonight. If Jenny and Rudy are still alive and are being kept somewhere like some fucking mines or an abandoned house, then they may end up dead by tomorrow morning."

Sofia turned her gaze away from his and focused on the window, shaking her head slightly as her eyes teared up.

"I'll get you the damn map," she said at last.

She left the room like a storm, slamming the door behind her.

After what seemed like an eternity, Sofia came back with a huge roll of paper wrapped around her arm.

"It's my dad's," she said, throwing the map to him. "He had it in his garage with a bunch of old stuff. I think it's from the fifties."

"Perfect."

Kevin unfolded the map completely on the bed, showing all corners of Heaven's Peak in detail.

"Which one are you looking for?" Sofia asked, peering over his shoulder.

"The coal mine. It's closed from the public so most likely it won't appear on commercial maps. However, this map shows where it is." Kevin pointed to the mine, at the foot of a mountain that surrounded the whole east side of the town. "The mansion appears here, too."

"And you plan to go and investigate, isn't it?" Sofia asked. "That doesn't sound like a very good plan if you ask me."

"It's our only lead."

"I still don't understand why you don't give this information to the police."

"Because it's not relevant, not yet at least. Worst-case scenario, we don't find anything, best case we find Jenny and Rudy. There is another possibility: that we find some tangible evidence, and then, yes, we would give it to the police for them to help us, not to do the work for us. Also, we shouldn't give this information to just anyone."

"What do you mean?"

"The people who questioned me the day Jenny disappeared, they are the ones we can trust. One was Lieutenant Cleyton, an asshole who wouldn't know what the fuck is going on if you put it in front of him. The other was an FBI agent. You see, when I was there, most of the officers seemed indifferent to the situation. At the end of the day, they only do their job, even if that job doesn't lead to any results. Agent James, however, does seem to want to put an end to all this. He's the only one we can trust at the moment."

"Why?" Sofia asked curiously.

"He's someone outside of everything that's going on, unlike the bunch of cops who've been investigating this for the last five years. Maybe he has a more of an open mind. I'm sure there's a supernatural aspect to all of this, and if I can prove it, then we have him on our side. That is why I'll take my camera. We'll also carry the walkie-talkies, batteries, and flashlights. We must be prepared for anything."

"I'm not going," Sofia said.

"What? Why not?" Kevin asked, surprised.

"What you're saying is crazy. I'm not going, and neither should you."

"Look, if you don't want to go, I understand. You're scared, and you have so much more to lose than me. But my sister is the only thing I have to live for, and I'm not going to sit here and wait for her to die."

"What about your dad?"

"He doesn't care about me. He spends all day drinking, and we barely see each other."

"Exactly, Kevin. Don't you think he needs you now more than ever?"

"He wasn't there when Jenny needed him, and neither was I. Now I'm making amends for that mistake."

"Nothing I say will convince you not to go, right?"

"I'm afraid not, Sofia."

Sofia stomped her foot and shook her head as she struggled to hold back tears.

"Then I'll go with you," she said, looking down at the floor.

"You don't have to," Kevin said, surrounding her with his arms.

"I just want to find my brother and make sure nothing happens to you."

Kevin held her against his body. With a sigh, he asked, "Where do you think we should go first?"

CHAPTER 20

⟡

Under the sun, near the stream, a group of birds rose in synchrony, frightened by the presence of an overdressed invader. Norman James grunted as he buried his foot in the ground, smearing his neat shoes, which would cost a fortune to clean, with mud. Clearly, he should have thought about what to wear before his expedition to the abandoned house, which no longer looked like a simple house in the light of day. Now that he could see it completely, he realized that it was much bigger than he remembered. It was the perfect place for a wealthy family until, according to what he had read, the owner murdered his entire family and disappeared.

James entered the crumbling structure. The only thing that seemed familiar was the smell of rot, the humidity and the same graffiti he had seen a few nights ago. However, the site looked and felt different. Now that all its details had been revealed, the oppressive atmosphere that had disturbed him that night was almost nonexistent. Even so, there was an aura of desolation that could make anyone's hair stand on end.

Almost without realizing it, he drew his gun and held it with both hands, the barrel pointing at the ground. He traversed the decaying corridors, where nature was already taking over. Grass grew in the crevices of the floor and tree branches squeezed through the walls as if they had entered with brute force.

James swallowed. The whole first floor seemed deserted. There was nothing but empty cans, trash, and grime. He went up to the second floor and recognized the door Sanders had come out of. He headed there, glancing over his shoulder from time to time, wary of each step. The room where Sanders had jumped out of the window was almost entirely empty. However, one detail made him take a closer look at the floor. A subtle trail of dark spots marched from the center of the room to the window.

James remembered that he had fired his gun as soon as he got inside. Maybe the spots were blood, but that didn't make any sense. How could someone not only survive a shot in the back but also let it pass like a scrape? Sanders should have been immobilized the moment the bullet struck his spine. Besides, there was no sign of him being injured at the interrogation room prior to being beaten by Cleyton.

He stood up and walked across the hall, where Sanders emerged. Right in the middle of the hall, a gaping hole gave way to the floor below, revealing a room he hadn't seen before. That room had a second larger hole that led to some kind of basement.

Cursing his luck, James holstered his weapon and jumped down. He rolled over his shoulder as he fell. All of his joints complained as he got up.

"Not as easy as it used to be," he whispered.

James leaned down into the second hole in front of him. He could scarcely distinguish anything thanks to the darkness, making it difficult to calculate the distance. He took the flashlight out of his belt and pointed it at the abyss. The torch drew a barely visible circle of light; however, he could see the ground, and that was a good sign.

He took a deep breath and jumped, landing in a puddle of water that splashed all the way to his shoulders. James spun around. The circle of light from his flashlight was now large enough to expose a wall in front of him. Mold stains ran all over the place, and the water was a grayish-green. The putrid smell filled his lungs until he grew dizzy.

James walked hesitantly into the basement. Come to think of it, it wasn't surprising that he hadn't seen the room with the hole on the first floor. That room didn't seem to be part of the house. It was as if they had been built the house on top of it. He cringed at the thought. The people who lived there were probably never aware that they lived on top of a vast open sewer system, or at least something that looked a lot like one.

The water flowed between his feet towards a tunnel in front of him. He got closer, careful where he stepped. He pointed the flashlight, his faithful companion, at the mouth of the tunnel. He couldn't see anything on the other side.

James put a hand on the sticky walls and withdrew it almost immediately. He had the feeling that he would catch some disease just by breathing. He gathered his courage and slid his fingers down the wall as he entered.

A few minutes went by before he stumbled across something different. It was an intersection of dome-shaped tunnels. On the ceiling, he could see a hole sealed by metal bars and the surrounding vegetation, through which the daylight filtered. He was in the sewers of Heaven's Peak.

How he had gotten there, he had no idea. Or rather, he didn't know how a hole in the abandoned mansion led there. Perhaps there was a well in its times of glory that had decayed, creating the hole he went through. Whatever the reason, the situation was looking better. Not because he was up to his knees in dirty water while wearing one of his bests suits, nor because of the certainty that if he let his guard down, he might get lost in that maze of tunnels. But knowing that, indeed, there was a place where criminals could hide and reach different parts of the town without being seen. It was brilliant.

Now all he had to do was tell the rest of the team at the station. He would take everything necessary for an expedition down there and wouldn't rest until he'd explored every corner of those tunnels.

The temperature seemed to fall several degrees at once, and he shivered. He felt compelled to go back, overwhelmed by a feeling of uneasiness.

James turned. There were about five dark silhouettes sheltered behind the columns of light coming from above. Their deformed faces were barely visible underneath the hoods they wore. It took him less than a second to recognize that those weren't their faces, but eerie masks of different colors and shapes. As different as they were, all of them had huge, menacing black eyes.

James drew his pistol and aimed it at the masked group.

"Put your hands up!" he shouted. The silhouettes didn't move an inch. "Put your fucking hands up, or I'll shoot!"

"You're not in a position to make demands," said one of the masked men, his voice muffled by the plastic that enveloped his face.

"I'm not joking!" James yelled, surprised at the group's confidence in front of a gun. He put his finger on the trigger and took the safety lock off. "This is your last warning!"

The hooded men approached him as if they hadn't heard. Some passed beneath the columns of light, revealing details of their masks. Some had horns, others twisted smiles, and one, the one behind all the rest, was white, with no features other than the black eyes, and it seemed to wrap the wearer's skull as if the plastic had burned and mixed with his flesh. He was also wearing a long black jacket that reached his knees.

Without hesitation, James raised the pistol and fired at the ceiling. The deafening shot rumbled through the tunnel. He expected what always used to happen in such situations—for everybody to get frightened and run away cursing in the opposite direction, or for one of them to pull out a gun and start shooting at random. Neither happened. It was something James had never witnessed in his entire career.

The masked men no longer walked but now ran towards him. With his heart in his throat, James realized he had no choice. He aimed at the one closest to him, right at the shoulder, and pulled the trigger.

A trickle of blood jumped from the suspect's shoulder, and he kept running, faster than before. James shot him again, this time in his chest. A red hole appeared where the masked man's heart must have been, but he just stepped back and shrugged it off before continuing his race.

James couldn't believe it. It was impossible. Sweat ran down his back beneath his suit, and both hands struggled to keep the gun steady.

The men were getting closer, all but the one in black, who stood behind them.

In a final attempt to test his own sanity, James fired again. The bullet struck in one of the mask's eyes, sending pieces of plastic flying, along with flesh and blood. The guy fell to the ground, only to rise again as if he'd just slipped.

James couldn't stand it anymore. He turned and ran in the opposite direction, aware that he wasn't going toward where he had first come. He had dropped down a hole, so he didn't have a way to climb up again even if he managed to get there, he'd rather run than be trapped in a room with them, but on the other hand, it meant he didn't know where he was going. The sound of their feet splashing behind him became louder and louder. Finally, he saw a light at the end of the long tunnel that grew brighter. His vision adjusted to the blinding light of day and he distinguished a thriving orange forest outside.

Just before he reached the exit, he glanced over his shoulder. A decision he would regret for the rest of his life.

One of the masked men was on all fours, suspended on the ceiling of the tunnel like a lizard. Another had what appeared to be two large appendages coming out of his back, like large, hairy spider legs.

James ran for his life.

CHAPTER 21

"Everything's prepared?" Kevin asked his partner.

"Are we really going to do this?" Sofia asked.

Kevin nodded. He strapped his backpack onto his shoulders and hung the flashlight from his belt. Everything seemed ready. Sofia gave him a furtive look of supplication, probably hoping he would change his mind, but he ignored her. The decision was already made.

"We should leave now so we can be back before it gets dark," Kevin said.

"Kevin," Sofia said.

"If you're going to try to convince me again not to go, then save your breath."

"That's not it. I think maybe, I don't know, shouldn't we be armed with something?"

"What do you suggest? A wooden bat? Or a crucifix? I don't think either will do much."

"My dad has a gun," she confessed. "It's in his safe. I know the combination. Maybe we should take it."

"I don't even know how to use a gun."

"Just point and shoot, right? Like a camera."

"I seriously doubt it's that simple. Besides, if we find Agent James or one of those fat ass cops, then what're we going to say, that we went hunting in the woods? I want us to make progress, not to waste time if the police finds us doing something suspicious."

"Why would they suspect us?" Sofia shouted. "We are the victim's families! Plus, you've only lived here for a few weeks. They can't think of you as a suspect. The disappearances have been going on for years."

"Maybe not, but we could be interrogated. And this expedition is a shot in the dark so we should avoid getting in trouble until we discover something solid."

Sofia crossed her arms, her eyes fixed on the floor. "Okay. Whatever you say."

She bolted out of the room, bumping into Kevin's shoulder. They didn't speak for the rest of the trip. Kevin walked with the map unfolded in front of him and Sofia following him closely. They entered the forest where they found the walkie-talkie. Once there, they continued on alternate paths, buried in seas of dead leaves.

As they stepped further through the trees, the silence became more intense. The birdsong and murmurs of wildlife faded away with every step until all they heard were the branches brushing against each other with the occasional breeze.

"How can you tell where we are on the map? This whole place looks exactly the same to me," Sofia whispered.

"The roads are almost invisible because it's been a long time since anybody used them, but if you pay attention, you'll realize that they are there. Also, the map points to some clearings that serve as a guide. If I'm not mistaken, we should find a river soon. From there, we'll continue uphill until we find a clearing at the foot of a mountain. That's the land that was sold to the mining company, and it should lead us straight to the entrance of the mines."

The sound of water making its way through the rocks soothed her. If she weren't standing and if her nerves weren't on edge, it would be enough to lull her to sleep. However, the sense of peacefulness didn't last long. As if he could see the future, Kevin's words came true, and Sofia calmed down a bit. He had been right about this, and she hoped with all her might that he was right about how the most likely outcome would be that they'd find nothing but a deserted mine. Although she always had better grades than him (she never saw him get anything higher than a C), she considered him to be much more intelligent.

"There it is," said Kevin.

Sofia glimpsed at the clearing in front of them. There was a rectangular structure built at the foot of the mountain with a huge dark tunnel as welcoming entrance. Sofia felt her heart race as she stepped on the cement. She turned to see that Kevin had paled. She waited for him to say that it was a bad idea, that they should go back and tell the police to take care of the rest, or at least get her father's gun and come back some other time. Instead, he kept walking towards the mouth of the mountain.

"This is crazy," she gasped, waiting for her companion to hear her.

Kevin pointed the flashlight into the darkness. Sofia imitated him, and they both entered the gloom. As soon as they stepped in the shadows, they found themselves surrounded by huge transport boxes and rusty barrels. The air was heavy. The walls joined the ceiling in a wide arch above their heads, yet despite the ample space, she couldn't help but feel suffocated. Their footsteps made a dull echo. She lowered her hand to Kevin's and squeezed it tightly. He responded in the same way.

They reached what appeared to be a giant wall that covered the entire tunnel, blocking the rest of the way. Kevin tugged at Sofia's hand, almost dragging her. To their right stood a metal door. His hand hovered over the knob and hesitated for a second. Sofia could guess what was going through his mind because it was the same thing that was going through hers: the fear that it was locked, or that the years had warped it so much it would not budge. However, the knob turned smoothly.

Sofia let out a sigh of anticipation. The door creaked in protest. They crossed the threshold and lit their way through a corridor decorated with signs displaying preventive measures and safety notices. One of them informed the employees about the eviction of the mines, detailing all the reasons why the mines were closed. Kevin flipped his flashlight over the letters. It basically said the same thing Mr. Wolf had told Kevin. However, something didn't seem to fit.

"What is it?" Sofia asked.

"This warning, it says the generators that ran electricity to the ventilation system would be shut down."

"So?"

"That's not what the teacher told me. According to him, the mines were shut down immediately after the fire was managed because people were afraid that the mine's gases would ignite and the whole place would explode. But this document says that there *was* a ventilation system installed. If that's the case, then why did they close it in the first place?"

"Maybe there was a failure in the ventilation system that caused the fire, and it was too risky to take another chance."

"Maybe." Kevin thought for a minute. "Actually, they closed this place as a precautionary measure, not because they had to, so I wonder if anyone would bother to keep this place running."

"If so, then you're right about what you said earlier. I don't think one single person could maintain this whole place alone."

Kevin was silent for a moment and gestured for Sofia to do the same. She nodded. He waited for his ears to start buzzing at the lack of sound, but instead, he heard the slight purr of a machine in the distance, confirming his suspicions. However, they had to see it with their own eyes to be sure. They hadn't come this far just to leave. As if she could hear what he was thinking, Sofia squeezed his hand again. He pulled her close to him and whispered in her ear:

"You can leave if you want, I'll keep going."

"I won't leave you alone."

He looked into her eyes and nodded, confirming what he was serious. He raised the flashlight and moved it around, revealing the walls of rust and decay. The couple continued zigzagging between barrels and rusty machinery. The dust in the air danced around their lights. The roar of the mysterious machine continued. Sofia bit her lip, their intertwined hands turning cold. They walked the rest of the corridor until they found an open area with platforms that served as elevators and metal fences. The breeze made the atmosphere much colder than should have been. It was unlikely that a current of air passed through such a closed place. That breeze had to be caused by some fan that made it circulate.

Kevin raised the flashlight to the ceiling and, in fact, they saw a fan spinning at full speed in the upper corner of one of the walls. That was the source of the purring sound.

"You were right," Sofia whispered in astonishment.

CHAPTER 22

Kevin had been wishing he were wrong. Suddenly, he felt the weight of his feet increasing, bringing him back to reality. Deep down, he had still held the slight hope that what he saw the night Jenny disappeared was nothing more than a nightmare, and he would wake up to eat breakfast with her, but no. Everything was real. Real people were disappearing, and real monsters lurked in the shadows.

He heard footsteps beside him. He tore the lantern from Sofia's hand and turned it off along with his. Sofia started to protest, but he covered her mouth before she could say anything. Silence fell over them after they were covered in darkness, but Kevin knew what he had heard.

The blackness was so dense that it made no difference whether their eyes were open or closed. Kevin let go of Sofia's hand and waited. All he could hear was the purring of the ventilation system.

Kevin stepped back gingerly until his back hit a wall. He groped in the dark for his partner but only found the cold touch of stone. There were footsteps again. They were lighter this time and moving away from him, first slowly, then accelerating to a trot. Sofia was running away. He wanted to scream, but his lips only trembled. He was sure there was someone there with them. He could feel a weight in the air that he didn't know how to explain. There was no way to rationalize it. Apart from the footsteps he thought he'd heard, there was nothing else that justified that feeling. He supposed it acted as a primitive sixth sense, an alarm that rang in his head when something went wrong but didn't know exactly what.

Against his better judgment, he raised the camera hanging from his neck, and took a picture. The light of the flash lasted only a fraction of a second, but it was enough to give a clear image of his surroundings.

To his left, he saw Sofia's golden hair disappear deep into the darkness. To his right stood a spectral figure wearing a white sweatshirt covered in blood. A hood concealed most of his head, but the light on the camera lit up what must have been his face, which was covered by a white mask with two black spots for eyes and a mocking smile from ear to ear.

Kevin's body reacted immediately and, by the time the flash faded, he was already running in the same direction as Sofia.

His feet seemed not to touch the ground as he ran, and he flailed his arms in all directions, expecting to hit something. Kevin put his hand on his belt, but couldn't find his flashlight or Sofia's. He must've dropped them the moment he saw the masked man.

Blind and desperate, Kevin took another picture. The flashlight illuminated his path, revealing that he was about to hit a wall, a metal staircase reflected on a platform to the side of it. In less than a second, he was again in shadows.

Guided by his memory, he darted toward the stairs. His hand hit the metal of the railing. Ignoring the pain, he used the railing to hoist himself up. He pressed the button on his camera again, which allowed him to see what appeared to be a booth. He slammed the door open and closed it behind him.

Kevin fell to the floor on his elbows, knees, and forearms. He stood up as fast as he could, drenched in sweat, his heart beating so fast it felt like the buzzing of a bee.

He gripped the camera with difficulty, feeling it slide between his trembling, sweaty fingers. He raised it to his face and pressed the button. Then it was clear he wasn't in a booth. Huge pipes were set up along the cave, entering and exiting the walls. At his side, giant machines he could only assume were generators roared in a chilling cacophony.

He blinked, and everything disappeared in a black veil. A knock on the door made him jump. Again, he used the camera to see what was happening. With horror, he caught a glimpse of the masked man making his way through a gaping hole in the middle of the door. Kevin screamed as he ran, following the direction of the pipes.

He stumbled a couple of times, but the memory of his surroundings was clear in his mind. It was as if, in a desperate effort to stay alive, his brain had etched every detail of what he saw in order to escape. It was incredible what the human body could do in a life-or-death situation.

Kevin stopped in his tracks and threw himself to the ground. Maybe that way he could buy himself some time before the hooded man found him. With the little courage he had left, Kevin tried to calm himself down and think of a way to get out. He couldn't stay there forever pretending to be dead. Where was he anyway? There were pipes and heavy machinery. If the bright image he had in his mind was accurate, then there was also a giant yellowish machine in the middle of the room with cables all over.

Probably one of the generators, he thought. If that was the case, then he was most likely trapped inside one of the power centers.

There was heavy breathing right next to him. Kevin stayed on the floor, holding his breath, afraid that the slightest sound would alert his pursuer. A drop of sweat slid down his forehead. The masked man was moving. His steps grew louder and louder.

Fuck it, Kevin thought, *I'm not going to die down here, not today.*

He jumped up and ran toward the generator, or at least where he remembered it being. His shoulder bumped against the cold metal as he heard the man in the white mask and black smile coming. Kevin ducked just in time to evade a punch. The masked man's fist crashed into the yellow metal and crushed it as if it was made of cardboard. Sparks jumped everywhere. The man yelled at the top of his lungs. It was a dreadful scream, nothing that could come out of a human being.

Kevin ran, avoiding some of the tubes and cables in his way. He was sure that his pursuer was right behind him. Deprived of his sight, his other senses had sharpened to such an extent that he could smell the sweat of his attacker behind him, combined with the smell of burning flesh. The machine's purring had stopped, and he could hear the beating of his heart.

He grabbed his camera tightly and took another photo. The flash showed that the door he had entered was right in front of him. Without wasting time, he threw himself at it. Kevin went out and down the stairs, tripping over the metal steps. His back crashed into the dusty ground. He got up in a blink and continued on his way, limping as he tried to regain his balance.

"Kevin?" It was Sofia's voice, somewhere in the distance.

"I'm here!" he shouted, panting. "I'm here, Sofia!"

"Where?" Her broken voice was on the verge of panic.

Using his camera to see, he barely discerned a figure in the distance, cornered against a wall.

"What was that?" Sofia yelled.

"It was me! Follow my voice and the light of the camera!"

Kevin took a picture every few of seconds as he drew closer to Sofia. A small hint of hope grew inside him. In the flash of the camera, Sofia's face turned from relief to horror as she looked over Kevin's shoulder. He grabbed her by the wrist and pulled her so hard that he almost made her fall, but she managed to keep her balance and keep up with him.

Finally, his hands, held high, clashed against a cold metal surface. Kevin followed it, praying for his memory to help him. He felt the opening of the door they had come from and he pulled with every fiber of his muscles. It budged a little, enough for them to go through. Sofia left first. He followed her but not before taking one last picture of the darkness they left behind.

They closed the door and ran. In the distance, they could see daylight at the end of the tunnel. Its heavenly glow was so unreal that Kevin wondered if he was still alive or if he was being received by death's embrace.

Above them, hundreds of bats flew in synchrony, as if scared by the same horrors they had endured. Sofia squeezed Kevin's hand as their feet hit the grass and a wave of fresh air hit their faces.

They didn't stop. They knew they would continue to run until they fainted or bumped into someone, whatever happened first.

CHAPTER 23

A blonde woman with excessive makeup was filing her nails behind the police station's reception desk. The tanned young man in front of her banged his fingers repeatedly against the counter and stared at her, waiting for a reply. She finished filing her little finger before answering.

"Agent Norman James is not here at the moment. I recommend you come back later."

"Are you deaf?" Kevin asked, trying not to raise his voice. "Because if you have a hearing problem, I'll repeat it for you. I have clues about a case that has been a pain the ass for the police for a long time, and I need to talk to Agent Norman James right now."

"Then I'm afraid you'll have to take a seat and wait because he's not here and we don't know when he'll arrive," the receptionist said, smoothing the rest of her nails.

"How can you not know when one of your agents is coming back? Did he escape? What the fuck are you talking about? From what you're telling me, he might be out drinking a fucking coffee, and you have no idea."

"Look, I really don't know what to tell you. I'm not a babysitter, so I apologize if I don't know everybody's exact location at all times."

Kevin ran his hand over his face in frustration. He knew that the law seriously punished people for hitting a cop but he wondered if the same applied to the receptionist. He had no choice but to wait like an idiot until the agent returned from his lunch break or wherever he was.

He thought about Sofia. The poor girl was still shaken by the time they had gotten home. Kevin had told her to rest while he developed the photographs and showed them to the agent. They had to wait a couple of hours for the pictures, and in the time they were together, neither spoke a single word to the other.

Even though he told her that they were safe and everything would be okay, he honestly didn't know if that was the case. He was afraid—no, he was terrified that the man they saw in the mines was still after them, which is why he didn't show any of the photos to Sofia once they were developed. The last one, in particular, had turned his blood cold.

"Any problems?" asked a voice over his shoulder.

Kevin recognized it instantly as Lieutenant Cleyton. If anyone knew about James's whereabouts, it would be him.

"Yes, Lieutenant, there's a problem," said Kevin. "I need to talk to agent Norman James as soon as possible."

"And why is that?" Cleyton asked. "What could be so urgent that you have to come here and yell at this lovely lady?"

"I have a clue about the missing people. I need to talk to him."

"Well, whatever you have to say to him you can tell me," Cleyton said, putting his arm around the boy's shoulder and taking him inside the station.

Cleyton escorted him past cubicles of people doing paperwork and cracking jokes. *So that's why they haven't solved a five-year-old case,* he thought. *All they do is waste time.* The lieutenant led Kevin inside an office where they sat down on opposite sides of the desk.

"I want to talk to Agent James," Kevin repeated.

"And the agent is not available right now." The lieutenant leaned over the desk. There was something off about him. Black veins peeked out of the lieutenant's neck. They were barely visible, but they were there. His eyes sunk in their sockets. Kevin thought it was strange for a man his age to have varicose veins, especially in his neck, and to look so…tired. "Come on, boy, spit out what you know."

"Don't take it personally, Lieutenant, but James is the one I want to talk to, so I'll wait."

"Oh, is that so? Since when you're so close to him?" Cleyton asked with a mocking smile. "Because, as far as I can remember, the last meeting we had wasn't very friendly."

"Just because we don't agree doesn't mean we don't want the same thing."

"I guess you're right." Cleyton looked down at the camera hanging from the boy's neck. He put his hands on the arm of his chair and stood up with a grunt. "Wait here for a second then. I have a couple of matters to attend to."

The lieutenant closed the door behind him as he left. Kevin waited for a couple of seconds as he heard his footsteps fade. When he was sure that Cleyton was gone, he got up, and slowly opened the door with the utmost caution. There was no one in the hallway. Kevin walked out.

Each door was engraved with the name of the office's occupant and their corresponding position: *Lieutenant Spencer Cleyton, Sheriff Thomas Gordon.* However, he didn't find any that read Norman James. Given his position and his involvement with the case, he should have one.

Kevin kept going until something at the end of the hall caught his eye. On a door that appeared to lead to the janitor's room, there was a piece of paper put up with duct tape. It read *FBI Agent Norman James.* Kevin smiled at the situation, but then he thought about how distant the agent's relationship with the rest of the police had to be. No wonder they didn't know where he was.

What if he was actually in there, though? Perhaps nobody knew or cared if he was there, or maybe they wanted to keep the credit for themselves if any clue came out? Kevin raised his hand to knock but stopped short. He didn't want to alert anyone else, so he decided to invite himself in. Worst-case scenario, it would be locked, but fate smiled on him. He walked into the office, making sure to lock the door behind him.

The only thing in that small room apart from dust and some boxes was a shabby desk right in the center of the room with a mountain of papers on top of it. Kevin imagined the painful process whereby the agent would have to pass just so he could sit in his chair without knocking over a tower of documents.

He focused on what he had to do. He took the pictures out of his jacket and remembered what the guy who developed them had told him: "Those are really disturbing." Kevin had lied, saying it was a horror-themed photographic project. The guy simply shrugged and said that he achieved his purpose.

Kevin had taken a lot of photographs when escaping the mine, most of them only showing dark corners or scenes blurred by movement. However, there were some that revealed just what he needed. They were so clear that not even a stubborn skeptic like Norman James could deny it.

One of them was of the man with the white mask. Judging by the way he was standing, he seemed to be ready to jump on them at the moment the flash blinded him. Another showed the enormous ventilation system Kevin had found. In the background, blurred fans were spinning in some of the cave's holes. The one he had taken as they left, however, was the winner. It showed the masked man running towards him. Behind the man, a grotesque creature that looked like a mixture between a bat, a skinned coyote, and a human was perched on the mine's ceiling. It was the same thing he'd seen the night Jenny was kidnapped. No way it was fake. James had to believe him now.

He grabbed a pen and wrote on a blank page:

"Here is the evidence that what I said is true. These photos were taken in the abandoned mines on the outskirts of the town. Please contact me as soon as you can.

DON'T TRUST ANYONE.

K."

He left all the photographs in an envelope next to the note and buried them under the pile of documents in such a way that it only jutted out a little. Once his task was completed, Kevin crept to the door and peeked out into the corridor.

What he saw petrified him.

In front of Cleyton's office were two cops, one on each side of the door, watching with crossed arms and frowns. They didn't seem to have the slightest idea that Kevin had already left the office. The Lieutenant surely had told them to keep an eye on him, but the idiots hadn't even bothered to check inside the office.

Kevin closed the door again, realizing the mistake he had made the moment he heard the thumping sound of the lock.

"What was that?" one of them asked.

"Don't tell me the agent already came back from his small expedition," said the other.

"I don't think so."

Kevin cursed to himself, his eyes quickly scanning the office. The handle began to move in a frenzy.

"Somebody's in there," one of the officers said in an unsuccessful attempt at a whisper. "Check Cleyton's office."

Now he was in deep shit. Kevin's first instinct was to head straight to the window. Outside, he could only see the branch of an oak brushing against the glass with the occasional breeze. Kevin looked down and calculated that he was probably around forty feet up, high enough to break something if he jumped.

They started to knock on the door.

"Hello?" It was Cleyton's rough voice, no doubt. "Come on, kid, get out of there! Let's not make a big deal out of this! Let's talk!" The knocking grew louder with every word. "I'll ignore the fact that you've just sneaked into a restricted area! Come on, kid, get out!"

His voice grew harsher and deeper until it almost sounded like a beast's groan. Kevin stepped back, convinced that Cleyton would kick the door down at any moment. He looked again at the tree branch hitting the window. Cleyton was still shouting for someone to give him a key to the office. Kevin swallowed. He didn't have time. It was all or nothing.

Kevin opened the window, put his foot on the windowsill, and reached for the nearest branch. He pulled it to himself. The wood creaked as the few remaining yellow and orange leaves fell. He reached out with his other hand and grabbed the branch. Now hanging from the tree, he tried to move forward, putting one hand in front of the other but barely managed to budge a little before his muscles began to scream. If he managed to get out of this mess in one piece, he'd start going to the gym.

Behind him, a crash startled him and almost made him lose his grip. To his surprise, a fist had pierced through the wooden door. It was Cleyton's.

Kevin only stared, gaping, as Cleyton took the lock off of the door and kicked it in. Never in his life had he seen such an extraordinary manifestation of brute force. Although he had seen people doing martial arts on television and breaking bricks and stuff like that, watching it in real life was an entirely different impression.

That wasn't what made his blood freeze. It was Cleyton's face, which had dark, bulging veins running from his neck to his cheeks. His eyes had turned black, giving him the gaze of a crow.

Kevin's fingers gave in to his weight. He fell and crashed into the ground at the foot of the tree. With a grunt, he stood up and ran to his house as fast as he could. He had to warn Sofia. He had to make sure she was safe. All the while he prayed for James to find his note with the pictures. He wouldn't have the time to go to Sofia's house. He had to warn her some other way, and tell her to find a safe place before the storm.

CHAPTER 24

⌒

Kevin threw the door shut behind him and pressed his back against it. He slid to the floor, gasping. He was sure that they hadn't followed him, but that wasn't exactly a victory. Sooner or later, they would come after him. At best, James would go with them, and Kevin could finally talk to him face to face. If that wasn't the case, then he might be in deep trouble. He had left the pictures on James's desk. All it would take was for someone else to find them and get rid of them. He would then be back to square one. He took a breath, as deep as his lungs allowed, praying to God that James saw the evidence before anyone else.

He took a second to rest, his heart pumping a thousand beats per second. He used the doorknob to prop himself up and walked with trembling legs into the living room. The house was empty. It was growing darker, even though it was barely five o'clock in the afternoon. Winter was just around the corner.

Kevin collapsed onto the couch, exhausted. He grabbed the telephone on the side table and dialed Sofia's number. The line seemed to ring forever before someone finally answered.

"Hello?" It was a female voice.

"Sofia, you're not gonna believe what I saw. Lieutenant Cleyton, I think he's one of them."

"This is Lia. What are you talking about?"

"Oh, shit."

"Hello to you too."

"Is Sofia there?"

"She's asleep. She was a mess."

"Wake her up, please. I need to tell her something very important."

"I'm not going to wake her up," Lia snapped. "Look, I don't know what the fuck you two were doing, but when she got here, she looked—different. She was scared and weeping. She was acting like the day Rudy, you know. So, as a favor, I'm going to ask that you don't put ideas in her head."

Kevin was starting to lose his temper. "Lia, what do you think—?"

"No. Listen, I don't want you to get together with Sofia again, okay? Look, I know about your sister, and you know about Rudy, so believe me when I tell you that I know how you feel and what you're going through, but—"

"Put Sofia on the phone," Kevin ordered.

"I won't. I think it's best for everybody if you stay away from us."

"Lia, please. You don't understand."

The beep on the other end of the line interrupted him. Lia had hung up. Kevin slammed down the phone.

"Damn it!"

He tried to dial again, but it only rang for a couple of seconds before he heard the horrifying beep signaling the line was unavailable. He had no choice but to go directly to the girls' house. Anyway, if Cleyton were looking for him, the first place he would try would be Kevin's house.

He had to hurry. The sun was setting. The snowstorm was predicted for that same night. Kevin put on his best winter jacket and stuffed all the clothes he could into a backpack with his camera, a flashlight, and batteries. He didn't want to be as unprepared as he was on his expedition to the mines. His stomach twisted at the thought.

He didn't know what he would do after meeting with Sofia and telling her what had happened. He had already tried to contact Agent James, which didn't work out as he'd expected. After seeing the lieutenant break a door with his bare fists, along his distorted face, he was in a dilemma. If he wanted to get in touch with James, it had to be behind Cleyton's back.

"Kevin."

The boy turned around. His father was on the other side of the room, next to the kitchen door. He wore a green jacket with a black stain on his chest. In both hands, he held an ax, covered in blood. John's eyes were wide open and fixed on him. Kevin got off the couch slowly, fearing that some sudden movement would be his last.

"Dad, what—what happened?" Kevin asked.

"You're not one of them, are you?" John's voice was broken. Sweat dripped down his forehead, and his arms trembled as they held the ax.

"One of them?"

"Don't be a smart-ass!" John yelled, raising the weapon above his head.

"I'm not, I'm not!" Kevin shouted with his hands held up. It took him some time to figure out what was happening. "You saw them too, didn't you? The men in masks."

"Masks?" John frowned. "I don't know what you're talking about."

"What are you talking about then?" Kevin asked, still not daring to lower his hands, even though his father had lowered the ax to his chest.

"The neighbors... they... I don't know what..."

"Tell me what happened," Kevin said, as calmly as possible.

"I went looking for Jeremy, the neighbor. Sometimes we go out to drink together, and I was going to invite him to have some beers today. When I arrived, the door was wide open. The house was a mess, as if it somebody had robbed it. I should've run away. I should've come back to the house and called the police, but, instead, I went in and... and..."

John lowered his head and closed his eyes, but that didn't stop the tears from coming.

"What did you see, Dad?" Kevin asked.

"Jeremy's wife was lying in the living room, what was left of her body, right next to the ax. Her head was in the kitchen, the expression she had... oh, God... the way she looked at me... was an expression of pure dread. I called Jeremy. That was my second mistake. I heard someone coming down the stairs. It was him. His eyes were black, empty. He had black veins popping out of his face. He smiled at me, a twisted smile. Next thing I remember was that I had the ax in my hand, though I don't know why. I guess it was pure instinct. He approached me, telling me to go with him. I don't know where the fuck he wanted to take me, but I wasn't going to listen to that psycho. When I said no, he threw himself at me, and I stuck the ax in his neck." John began sobbing. He was shaking all over, reliving the moment. "The son of a bitch stood there like it was nothing and spat, or threw up, on me. I don't know what the fuck it was, but it was rotten and black. It covered

189

my face, I even think I swallowed a little. He dropped to the floor. I was there for God knows how long, I guess trying to process what had happened. I grabbed the ax and pulled it off his neck. I hated to see him like that. He was my friend."

"And then what?" Kevin asked, his lips trembling.

"I went out to get help but found no one. It was as if everyone had disappeared. I knocked on the neighbor's doors and peered through their windows. I would swear I heard people inside, but they probably were as terrified as I am. I came back and found that Jeremy was no longer there. How is that possible, Kev? How do you stick an ax in someone's neck and they just walk away?"

Kevin didn't know how to answer. Some of the details caught his attention: black eyes and prominent veins, just like Cleyton. Was it a disease? If so, it made sense for it to be contagious. He thought of the black stain on his father's jacket, that dark goo.

"How long ago did that happen, Dad?"

"A few hours ago, then I decided to come here and hide. I was convinced you didn't make it."

A loud bang somewhere in the distance made the windows shake. It sounded like an explosion.

What the fuck is going on? Kevin wondered.

"How do I know you're my son?" John asked, stepping forward.

"What are you talking about, Dad? Of course, I'm your son."

"Prove it."

John moved closer and closer, the ax now rising over his shoulders. Kevin's legs felt like rubber.

"Dad, calm down."

"Prove to me who you are. Prove it!" John demanded, waving the ax above his head.

Kevin didn't know what to say. His mind ran through a thousand possible scenarios. He thought of spelling his full name, telling him about his mother's death or the date they arrived at Heaven's Peak, but in all those situations he imagined himself ending up with the edge of the ax between his eyebrows.

"Dad..."

His words were interrupted by the sound of sirens from outside the house. The unmistakable red and blue lights filtered through the window. Kevin thanked all the gods while his father was still trying to process what was happening. Driven by instinct, Kevin bolted for the door and ran across the yard to the cop stepping out of the squad car. The cop spun and pulled the pistol from his belt. Kevin raised his hands immediately as he stopped short.

"Don't shoot!" Kevin shouted.

"Put your hands in the air!" the cop yelled, pointing at him. He turned his attention to John. "Drop the ax and raise your hands!"

His father stopped, his eyes fixed on the cop and a tight grip on the ax, refusing to let go.

"Dad, please, do as he says," Kevin begged.

John walked forward.

Kevin stepped in between them, not thinking clearly. There was a trigger-happy cop in front of him and a psychotic man with an ax behind him. Yet there was no way he could let his father die, not like this.

"Step aside," the cop commanded.

Kevin shook his head. There was no way out of the situation

"Look out!" the cop yelled.

Kevin turned and saw the edge of the ax shine over him. He dodged the metal by a mere inch and stumbled to the ground. John ran toward the officer, ax held high like a warrior heading into battle.

The cop fired twice. Two red holes appeared in John's torso, one in the chest and the other in the stomach. Kevin watched in horror as his father's body dropped to the ground. The ax fell on the freshly pruned lawn, its green leaves painted red.

"No!" Kevin yelled as he stood back up. "No! Why did you do that? You fucking maniac!"

The cop pointed the gun at him. "Do you want to be next?"

"Officer," started Kevin, on the brink of panic. "Please, this is just a misunderstanding. I'm not dangerous."

The officer's hands couldn't hold the pistol steady. His eyes showed that he had endured several surprises that day and he'd been trying to make sense of the world ever since.

"I saw a fourteen-year-old girl bite her own father's ear off, so don't you dare—"

"Look me in the eye, Officer. Do I really look like the kind of person capable of that?"

"Don't try to trick me! Things are not what they seem, not today. I learned that the hard way."

"You're right, Officer, you're right. I'll go with you, okay? Just put the gun down."

From among the black trees around them came a growl, a guttural sound so deep and horrifying that no animal could've made it. Kevin recognized it instantly. He started to walk quickly towards the officer, his heart ready to pound out his chest.

"We have to get out of here, quick."

"Keep your hands up!" the cop yelled, waving his pistol at Kevin.

"No! We don't have time for this shit! We have to get out of here!"

The cop stepped closer. "I'm not saying it again."

Kevin raised his hands.

"Neither will I. We have to go. Take me to the station, wherever you want, but make it fast."

The radio of the police car awoke, like a child in the middle of the night waiting for the most inconvenient time to wake his parents. From it came the voice of Lieutenant Cleyton, raspy, deeper than usual, and with the rage of a thousand demons.

"Attention all units! We are receiving reports of outbursts of violence throughout Heaven's Peak! If you see a civilian carrying a weapon, shoot to kill! These people are dangerous! Don't be fooled! I repeat: shoot to kill!"

The officer's gaze was glued to the car, his eyes open so wide they seemed ready to come out of their sockets. In a fraction of a second, the officer and Kevin made a decision. The officer turned and opened fire on the boy just as Kevin darted to the side of the road, to a hill covered by a row of trees. Kevin felt the hot air mere inches away as bullets flew past him. His shoulder hit the ground as he rolled downhill until his back crashed against a pine.

Kevin crawled across the damp earth and pulled himself up, his feet struggling to regain their balance. Pieces of wood and dirt jumped as the bullets hit the ground. All he heard was a buzzing that pierced his ears. He knew that gunshots were loud, but he'd never imagined how deafening they were, especially on the other side of the barrel.

His vision blurred. He didn't know exactly where he was going. He just ran. Surrounded by trees in the darkness, illuminated only by the faint blue and red flicker behind him, Kevin began to zigzag. He was sure the cop couldn't see him, but considering how close the bullets were, the cop must've had a very good idea of his position. His feet were soaking wet as he stepped in the mud, his arms bumping against branches constantly, about to stumble and crash face-first into the ground.

Once the buzzing in his ears stopped, he could hear one shot after another echoing in the forest until suddenly there was dead silence. He continued his marathon as far as he could until his sides began to complain and his lungs screamed for air. He put his hand against the trunk of a tree and regained his composure. His head felt light, dazed. He looked around, unable to see anything more than a few feet away. As he caught his breath, he found it was getting harder to breathe. Even though he took great puffs of air, he felt like suffocating. It was as if the blackness of the forest had enclosed him in a metal box under a padlock and flushed the key. He broke into a cold sweat and fell to his knees.

He had to go to Sofia's house as soon as possible.

CHAPTER 25

⁓

Sofia filled her hands with water and washed her face. She looked up at the mirror. It had been a while since the last time she took care of her appearance, and it was starting to show. Her abs were noticeable, along with her ribs. She had probably lost about twenty pounds in the last couple of months. Without further examination into her poor image, she let her hair down and decided to go to bed. But something bumped against her window, making her jump. She turned on the light.

Sofia put her back against the wall and tiptoed to take a peek out the window, making sure she wasn't in the line of sight of whoever was outside. A small stone bounced off the glass. Someone with a hood was crouching in her garden looking for another rock to throw. Sofia covered her mouth to avoid screaming as she remembered the masked man back in the mines. The hooded man straightened and, thanks to the streetlight, she recognized Kevin's face, and she was overwhelmed with a massive sense of relief. With a sigh, Sofia went down to the living room.

As she grabbed the doorknob, she remembered that she only had on a loose shirt and short shorts. Before she could go back and get dressed, the door swung open. She jerked her head back to avoid breaking her nose. Kevin jumped inside, his eyes swollen and his face red. His clothes were covered with dirt and what looked like blood.

"Sofia, are you okay?" Kevin whispered.

"Are *you* okay?" she asked, perplexed. "What happened to you?"

"Everyone in town went crazy."

"What?"

"Let me spend the night at your house."

"No! Are you crazy? My parents will kill me if they see you here."

"Sofia, please, I need you. The police are after me."

Sofia's eyes widened. "What kind of mess did you got yourself into?"

"I'll explain it upstairs, okay? Just let me stay."

She folded her arms, taking in a deep breath. "Oh, God. Kevin, come on, hurry up before anyone sees you."

She grabbed him by the hand and led him into her room. Kevin sat on the bed and covered his face with both hands while Sofia locked her door. She sat down beside him and put her hand over his, demanding with a pleading look that he tells her what was going on, and Kevin did. He described how he sneaked into James' office, got home to find his dad threatening him with an ax, and then the mishap with the cop, who didn't hesitate to kill his father.

"Did the cop shoot at you too?"

"Yes," Kevin answered, avoiding her gaze. "I was scared. I was so scared."

"Come here," Sofia replied, putting her arms around his shoulders. He came closer to her, and she hugged him tightly.

Kevin buried his face in Sofia's shoulder and let out a sob. Sofia's heart shattered. She opened her mouth to say something, but closed it again. There was nothing she could say to make the situation better. All she could do was hold him and not let go. This brave guy whom she admired so much had become a child who needed her.

"I don't know what to do," Kevin moaned, his breathing ragged as he wiped his face with his hand. "This is all fucked up. I can't go on."

Sofia gently pushed him away from her, lifted his chin with her finger and looked into his bloodshot eyes. "We can't give up now. You said it yourself. We have to keep going no matter what, for the sake of our families."

"It's too much, it's too much."

"Maybe it is too much for you and me to handle, but we can still count on Agent James."

"I guess you're right."

"Of course I'm right. I have to be the voice of reason every once in a while."

Kevin smiled. "So, what do you suggest?"

"Let's go to the police station again to see if we can talk to James. I'll be backing you up, and if anything sounds suspicious, I'll be your alibi."

"No!" he shook his head. "We can't go back to the station. We can't. Cleyton could still be there and... Fuck, you didn't see what I saw. Going back there is not an option."

"Our priority is James, so don't worry about Cleyton. We can find the Agent if we work together."

"You're the best, did you know that?"

"Yes, I know."

They laughed. She motioned for him to lower his voice in case they woke up someone in the house. Kevin nodded and put his hand on her cheek. Sofia was surprised but didn't stop him; instead, she brought her lips closer to his.

CHAPTER 26

Cleyton parked in the police department's lot after broadcasting his message to all the squad cars in town. He opened the trunk to retrieve the pump action shotgun and a belt full of ammunition. Ready for action.

Whoever Lieutenant Spencer Cleyton once was found himself drowning in a dark sea inside his own subconscious, screaming for help. His body was now dominated by another being, a strong, agile and cunning entity.

The creature wearing Cleyton's skin entered the station and received a greeting from the blonde receptionist talking on the phone. She didn't get to finish telling her friend how boring her job was before her head was blown up into a thousand pieces. From the mouth of the shotgun came a wisp of smoke that was dissipating as Cleyton, or rather the entity in Cleyton's body, moved towards its next target.

Now that most of the officers on duty were scattered around Heaven's Peak, tending to the dozens of emergency calls that had been pouring in over the last couple of hours, it was the perfect opportunity for what the creature had in mind.

He, or rather It, kicked the reception door open. There were barely a dozen officers in their cubicles that, alerted by the unexpected blast, stood up expectantly. The majority of their expressions changed from confusion to disbelief as Cleyton pointed the shotgun at the officer standing right in front of him, Reyes, and pulled the trigger.

Reyes' torso exploded in a mixture of blood, bones, and gunpowder. By the time his body touched the station's neat floor, the officer was already dead.

Amid the screams, several cops instinctively took their guns out but hesitated. It took a couple of seconds while their minds processed that the person who had just murdered one of their colleagues in cold blood was the lieutenant.

Cleyton took advantage of that fleeting moment, to shoot the next officer, Velázquez, who was on his right. The shot disintegrated part of his shoulder and face, spraying the white wall with red.

Just as Cleyton reloaded the shotgun, a bullet pierced his chest. He felt no more than a slight bump. He aimed at whoever made the attack and fired without hesitation. Another rain of bullets rushed towards him and, as if they were practice targets, he took out each and every one of the officers.

Once his work was done, and most of the station was decorated with red stains and corpses in blue uniforms, Cleyton made his way to the sheriff's office.

He slammed the door open. The big man in his sixties was at his desk, his fingers buried in the arms of the executive chair. The sheriff jumped up, shaking, his eyes locked on Cleyton with pure dread. Without wasting any more time, the Lieutenant raised his weapon at his former boss and executed him.

Now there was only one person left on his list: Norman James.

CHAPTER 27

James had arrived just fifteen minutes earlier. After that frightful experience in the sewers, he wanted nothing more than a good shower and to take refuge in his hotel room while the storm passed, but he couldn't. A small voice in his mind insisted that he should return to the station and warn everybody about the horrors he had witnessed, but how could they believe him? No one would take something like that seriously. Most likely they would think he was taking drugs with the neighborhood kids.

He had no choice but to persuade Cleyton to organize an expedition to the place, with several men to cover them and the necessary equipment to confront the masked men.

However, he found the station almost empty. There were no more than half a dozen men in the place. When he asked where they had all gone, they merely told him that the town had gone to shit during the last few hours. People were raiding shops, families killing each other and fires burning throughout the town.

The agent wondered if it was just a case of massive hysteria. But it didn't make sense, there had to be some sort of trigger for such madness. Although the news had recommended buying supplies and staying indoors for a couple of days, it didn't deserve such a drastic reaction.

He thought about what he went through only a couple of hours ago and wondered if he too had become part of that collective psychosis or, worse if what he witnessed was a real supernatural force that might have something to do with the behavior of the townsfolk.

Willing to get to the bottom of the matter, James headed for the sheriff's office.

"I need to talk to you," James said to the sheriff, who was smoking a cigar while talking on the phone.

"I'll call you later, Morris," Gordon said before hanging up the phone. "What do you need, Agent?"

"I need an explanation," James began. "According to the reports, the police made an exhaustive search of the entire town and surrounding areas after the first victim disappeared, and the procedure was presumably repeated with each victim. However, I have reasons to doubt the veracity of those reports."

"Really?" Gordon raised an eyebrow in mock interest. "And what makes you doubt the reports?"

James took a deep breath. There was no easy way to say it.

"Because I went on a small expedition to an abandoned mansion on the outskirts of Heaven's Peak, a site that should have been investigated by local authorities, especially considering that it is the perfect place for criminal activities."

"Well, I'm informing you that those searches did take place. I supervised each one of them myself." Gordon got up from his chair and moved closer to James with each word until he was mere inches from him.

"Then I'd like to see the full report of Jennifer Miller's search because I wasn't invited, even though I was here when it happened. I want to see dates, names, and places."

"Agent, would you be so kind as to share your experience with me? Considering how much it has affected you, it is surely something I should know in detail."

James hesitated. He wanted to wait until the moment was right. Once he had some sort of evidence or had convinced Cleyton to conduct the search, he would then tell him what had happened. That was the plan at least, but the words came out of his mouth as if his lips had a life of their own.

"I went to the mansion. I found a hole that led to the sewers. There was a group of masked people waiting for me there. I was surrounded, so I told them to retreat. They tried to attack me, and I shot one in the chest, where his heart should've been. He didn't even blink. He wasn't wearing any kind of bulletproof vest or anything like that. I shot again, and the same thing happened. I got out of there as fast as I could."

"You're starting to sound like a nut job, Agent."

"So I started to think, what if the boy, Kevin Miller, was right?" James asked. Gordon ran his hands over his head, frowned, and opened his mouth to reply, but James interrupted him. "Then I remembered Sanders. He was wearing the same kind of mask as the rest of those freaks. Even though it seemed that he smashed his head against the sink, the coroner told me it was more like it was crushed. So if they, somehow, can shrug off bullets, then maybe they also have enough strength to crush somebody's skull."

Gordon's expression remained cold, almost apathetic.

"So you don't think the boy killed himself?" he asked.

"At first I thought there was foul play involved, but when I saw what those…people could do, I started thinking that maybe Sanders did kill himself. Maybe, instead of using the sink, he just used his bare hands. Which brings me to my next point. A few hours ago we found the bodies of Jack and Margery Jensen. She seemed to have broken her neck while he was found in the same condition as Sanders. Also, their son, Robert Jensen, is missing. He's our best lead."

Gordon didn't seem affected at all by this speculation, which took James by surprise.

The sheriff gave a deep pull on his cigar. "I don't know what you've been smoking, agent, but it was cheap shit. Besides, as far as I understand, no officer in the area reported seeing a hole that led to the sewers."

"Because the only way to get to it is from the second floor. And I can assure you that none of your fat-ass officers even bothered to go up the stairs."

"Choose your next words carefully, agent," Gordon said, crossing his arms.

"I need to talk to Lieutenant Cleyton."

Gordon turned and waved his hand in the air.

"The lieutenant is not available at the moment. Leave him a message after you hear the beep."

"Then I'll wait," James said flatly.

He left Gordon's office and went to his own. While he waited for the lieutenant to arrive, he could start finding out as much as possible about the mansion and the town's sewer system. He got in his office, and cleared his desk of the dozens of documents and folders. A dry sound caught his attention. A piece of paper fell to the floor. It had handcrafted calligraphy on the front, and below was a pile of recently developed photographs.

James picked up the note and read it. He couldn't believe it. The mines. It made sense since the mines were abandoned just like the mansion. However, as far as he knew, just being there was dangerous. It didn't take him long to figure out the meaning of the K at the end.

"Kevin."

Although the boy was stubborn and disrespectful, he was brilliant. A smile flickered across the agent's face without him noticing. Now he had the evidence he needed for the expedition.

Just as he stood up and put the pictures in his suit, he heard a blast from outside. The sound was unmistakable. It was from a pump action shotgun, and it was terribly close. Just thinking about what might have happened froze his blood.

He heard it again, and then a third time. Within a couple of seconds, a cacophony of shots echoed through the station. They were coming from right outside his office.

James pulled out his revolver. There were more shots, coming closer each time. He felt a pressure in his chest that increased with each bang. He lay down on the floor to see under the door and saw feet in front of the sheriff's office. Another shotgun blast made him jump.

The feet turned, they were heading for James' office. The agent, blinded by the adrenaline rush that ran through his body, opened the door and aimed his revolver directly where the killer's face would be. His finger stilled on the trigger.

"Cleyton."

The lieutenant's eyes were all black and sunken in their sockets. The veins of his neck spread over his face, giving him the appearance of a walking corpse. In his hands, he held out a shotgun aimed straight at James.

"It's a shame that it has to end this way, agent." Cleyton put the shotgun on his shoulder. "I must admit I respected you and, to a certain extent, I liked you."

"Drop the gun right now, Cleyton, or I'll shoot!"

The moment he let those words slip, he realized they wouldn't do any good. The lieutenant had several holes in his clothes proving that James wasn't the first to try to stop him. Cleyton was one of *them*.

The lieutenant pulled the trigger. The only sound was an empty click. James lunged at Cleyton, ramming him with all his weight as the lieutenant prepared to reload the shotgun. They both crashed to the ground, with the gun between them. James put his revolver to Cleyton's temple and fired. A trickle of blood spattered his face. Cleyton, instead of remaining immobile on the ground, uttered a spine-chilling cry. It was the roar of a beast James had never heard in his life.

Cleyton shoved the agent to the side and slammed him into the wall. As the lieutenant tried to get up, James fired again, this time directly at Cleyton's eye. The dark basin exploded in a mixture of blood and a black liquid, a piece of flesh hanging along his cheek. Cleyton let out another howl of pain as he dropped the shotgun.

James grabbed it and stood up. The lieutenant had barely had time to put a bullet in his barrel before James pushed him down, so he had a single shot to spare. It was better not to waste it.

James lunged through the hallway, taking cover behind one of the cubicles. Cleyton pulled out his pistol and started shooting in all directions. The thunderous shots blew holes in the walls and floor near James. He mustered enough courage to peek around a corner. Cleyton was walking towards him with the gun raised. James stared down the hallway that led back to his office; he wanted to run to the door and lock himself inside, but with Cleyton on the path, he would end up with a bullet in the head and his brains scattered on the floor.

James zigzagged between the cubicles with his head down. The gunshots started again. Chunks of wood and pieces of tiles flew apart as bullets hit them. A warm sensation ran down his arm as he entered one of the cubicles.

He looked at his bicep and saw that it was stained red. He heard the lieutenant's footsteps edging closer. James waited, his back against the cubicle wall, sitting on the floor with the shotgun held high. As soon as he saw a movement out of the corner of his eye, he took a shot.

Cleyton had peered out, ready to put a bullet between the agent's eyebrows as the blast of the shotgun propelled him backward. The lieutenant's body fell on top of a table, knocking down everything on top of it.

James ran toward the exit, covering his wound with his hand. Once he reached the door, he couldn't resist looking back. Cleyton was getting off the desk with difficulty as if he were trying to recover from a hangover. A shotgun blast at point blank range did nothing more than stun him. James ran as fast as he could into the parking lot; he reached his undercover car, panting as he crashed against the hood. He got in, squeezing his arm to keep from losing more blood, closed the door and put his bloodstained hands on the wheel.

As soon as he turned on the engine, something jumped on top of the hood. A creature with a deformed face threatened him by exposing a row of sharp fangs. It seemed to have a man's body, but its skin looked like that of a dead dog without fur. Its eyes were black like the night. The monster dug its sharp claws into the windshield, mere inches away from James' eyes. The agent stepped on the accelerator with all his might. A thunderous blow hit the roof of his car. James aimed his revolver at the ceiling and emptied the cartridge. There was a nerve-wracking shriek, and James saw in his rearview mirror another monster rolling on the ground behind him.

He moved the wheel to the right, scraping the door against the parking lot wall. Sparks flew everywhere. The creature still on his hood struck the windshield with its claws. James sped up as fast as he could and planted his foot on the brake. The creature flew into the street, rolling across the pavement. James reversed the car back and turned in the opposite direction.

Behind the mask

CHAPTER 28

A shrill scream startled them. Sofia's face looked pale even under the faint silver glow coming from the window. Kevin froze.

"D-did you hear that?" she asked, her lip trembling.

"Of course I heard it." Kevin's eyes widened, and his senses sharpened.

"I think it came from downstairs."

"Stay put," said Kevin as he got out of the bed.

"What? No, you can't leave!" she insisted, grabbing his arm.

"Don't worry, I'm just going to make sure—"

There was a second, terrified cry.

"No! Please, stop!" a woman shouted from the living room.

Kevin knelt to face Sofia. "What is the combination for your dad's safe?"

"The gun," Sofia stammered, her face white as the moon. "It's, uh, shit... three, four... six... Two, I think. No, no, no, six, seven."

"Three, four, six, seven," Kevin repeated.

"It's behind his closet. I'll go with you." Sofia rose to her feet.

"No! Call the police, tell them what's going on and hide."

"Are you crazy?"

"Just listen to me! Look what happened the last time you didn't."

He didn't mean to be so harsh on her, but they didn't have time to argue. Sofia seemed surprised at his response, almost offended. She gave him an I-can't-believe-you-said-that look.

"There's a phone in my parents' room," she finally said.

Kevin grabbed her by the hand, and they peered out the door. A dim light was coming from the living room. The silence was dense as smoke. They both snuck out of the bedroom, paranoid that the mere beating of their hearts would give them away.

They managed to enter her parents' room without making any noise. Kevin's eyes soon adjusted to the darkness. There was nobody there, and the place was a mess as if they had left in a hurry. Sofia opened the closet and moved all the clothes aside like a curtain. On the wall was a safe with a keypad.

"It's too dark," she said in a low voice.

Kevin cursed his luck. The flashlight was in his jacket back in Sofia's room. He leaned into her ear and whispered to her not to move until he returned. Before she could protest, he headed down the hall again, silent as a cat. A shadow slid on the wall toward the stairs, it looked like the leg of a giant spider. Kevin shuddered.

He threw himself into the room without any regard to how much noise he made. When he found the jacket lying on the floor beside the bed, he grabbed it and began to pat it frantically. Kevin finally felt the steel of the flashlight and took it out of his pocket. He ran back to the other bedroom, afraid of looking at the stairs, and locked the door as soon as he entered. The door wouldn't make any difference if it was one of those monsters, but it comforted him a little.

He went to Sofia and turned on the flashlight. She blinked at the blinding light, reached out and put the combination. The safe opened.

What was inside made Kevin doubt the existence of a benevolent and merciful God.

"That's not a gun," Sofia gasped.

"Looks like a fucking toy."

All his efforts had gone down the drain. Inside, there was nothing but jewelry and a flare gun right in the center. Kevin wondered who would keep something like that in a safe. He looked at Sofia, and she seemed to read his thoughts.

"Maybe he put it here to keep Rudy from playing with it," she said.

It didn't matter the reason. Kevin grabbed the gun and the three flares at its side. He put one in the gun and the other two in his jacket. Just imagining what might be happening outside, he felt the urge to jump out the window, to run as far away as possible without looking back, but he couldn't leave Sofia alone. He almost lost her once. He wasn't going to let it happen again.

He gestured for the girl to go to the phone that was on her parents' bedside table. She nodded. Kevin gathered all the strength of will he had left and wondered if he was suicidal as he left the room and went down the stairs, gun raised as if it could intimidate anybody. He took each step with caution trying to ensure that the wooden steps wouldn't squeal under his weight. Kevin stopped dead at the horrifying sight before him.

Just as he set foot at the bottom of the stairs, a delicate female hand appeared with a brilliant wedding ring still on its finger. Freshly painted crimson-red nails blended in with the pool of blood around them. Kevin let out a gasp as the fingers of the severed arm still twitched. He had the urge to vomit, lightheaded and under the impression that the world around him was spinning out of control.

Trying to keep his composure, Kevin followed the trail of blood. The room seemed painted by an abstract artist who was very fixated on the color red. The walls, furniture, floor, even the ceiling were all stained. In the center of the room was what remained of Sofia's mother. He deduced that the incomprehensible pink mass, separated from the rest of the body, was her head, thanks to the remnants of long blond hair. Beside him, her torso lay apart from her legs and the other arm, twisted in such a way that it seemed like she was trying to put herself together again. A sense of vertigo seized him. He closed his eyes and brought his hand to her mouth as he tried to swallow back the vomit that had already risen to his throat.

There was no trace of Sofia's father, but Kevin didn't want to find him either.

Sobs coming from the kitchen alerted him. He approached slowly, trying not to slip in the pool of blood that covered the floor. His shaky hands could barely hold the flare gun. Kevin peered into the dining room and saw him, the same guy that he had seen in the mines, recognizing the same white sweater soaked almost entirely in blood, his smiling mask and the long hair that came out of his hood. Lia crawled on the floor in front of him, an open wound on her forehead, tears on her face and an expression of absolute terror. The man turned over his shoulder as if he felt Kevin's presence.

Kevin stepped back, aiming the pistol directly at the masked man's chest but keeping his gaze on the ground. He couldn't bear the sight of those seemingly empty black eyes. However, what happened next made his blood run cold.

The man raised a hand to his face, stripped off his mask and took off his hood, revealing a tangle of dirty hair. Despite the sunken eyes, dark gaze and veins that seemed about to explode on his face, Kevin recognized him.

"R-Rob? What the fuck?"

"Kevin!" he exclaimed. His voice sounded guttural, like an animal trying to speak. "What a pleasant surprise."

Rob's demonic smile had ripped his cheeks open, showing a row of fangs.

"What the hell happened to you?" Kevin asked, his words trembling as much as his body.

"I received a gift from someone much bigger than me, bigger than all of us. It's a bliss. You should join us."

"And look like that?"

"Stronger, faster. You would be a valuable asset. Considering how long it takes for the children to incubate, we need more like you and me."

"What the fuck are you talking about?"

"Shoot him!" Lia shouted. "What are you waiting for?"

Rob turned and grabbed her by the neck. His nails had turned into long claws that pointed straight at her jugular.

"Shut up, you fucking bitch!" Rob ordered. His distorted voice echoed throughout the house.

"I'll go with you." Kevin left the flare gun on the floor and kicked it into the hallway. He raised both hands above his head in surrender. "I'll join whatever fucked-up cult you're part of, just don't hurt her."

Rob released Lia, and she collapsed on the floor, coughing as if she were about to spit out a lung. The monster using Rob's body again showed off his putrid smile. Although his eyes were almost completely black, Kevin could see a blue hoop where his pupils must have been, and they were looking straight at Kevin.

He could feel his heart coming out of his chest as Rob approached him with those huge teeth. A thread of saliva ran from his red lips to his chest. Rob reached his claws toward him, grabbed him by the shoulders and threw him to the floor. Kevin screamed as Rob climbed on top of him with a shark-like smile.

Behind them, a tearful scream of panic swept across the room. Rob's neck twisted back in an inhuman way, all the bones in his back cracking in unison as he fixed his gaze in the opposite direction. In the middle of the room stood Sofia, kneeling in a pool of blood beside her mother's mutilated body. Her face contorted in a grimace of pure, agonizing pain. The girl began to sob as she shook her head from side to side frantically, refusing to believe what was happening before her eyes.

"Sofia!" Kevin yelled. "Get out of here! Grab Lia and leave, both of you!"

Rob turned back to him, opened his hideous jaws, and spat a black substance on him. Kevin felt as if a bucket of boiling water had been thrown into his face, an indescribable pain running through his body equivalent to each and every one of his bones breaking at once. An unbearable sting went down from his throat to his stomach. He could feel his organs burning from the inside.

He screamed as loud as he could, kicking and struggling to push off the monster on top of him. A hump grew out of Rob's back until his sweater ripped apart revealing four appendages, two on each side, black, hairy and sharp like spider legs.

Rob laid two these appendages on the floor, and the other two on the walls, lifting his body into the air. Kevin rolled to the side and stood up. At that very moment, Lia threw herself to the ground, grabbed the flare gun, aimed at the beast, and pulled the trigger.

A crimson flash burst out of the mouth of the gun, flooding the room with red light and landing on Rob's back. He gave a monstrous shriek and arched his back.

"Let's go!" Kevin yelled as Rob fell and writhed on the floor, wrapped in flames.

Sofia hadn't finished assimilating what was happening by the time Lia grabbed her by the arm and forced her to rise. Kevin ran in the opposite direction, picked up one of the small tables and threw it into the living room window. Thousands of glass shards flew through the air. Before jumping through the window, Kevin turned to see Rob standing on his deformed appendages, his charred skin melting into pieces embraced by the fire. His monstrous jaw let out a grunt.

Kevin's knees dropped on the wet lawn and pieces of broken glass. He landed with his hands to the front, preventing his face from hitting on the ground. Behind him, the two sisters jumped, holding hands. He held out his hand to help them but was surprised to see Lia, instead of reaching out her hand, giving him the flare gun.

"Run!" she shouted and took Sofia with her, almost dragging her in the opposite direction.

Kevin understood what Lia was trying to do and, much to his dismay, he followed through with her plan. Rob probably would chase him, so Lia decided not to risk the life of her sister, the only member of her family left alive, by staying with Kevin. That's why she gave him the gun so that he could defend himself the moment Rob came after him. Kevin ran towards the main avenue and turned to see the deformed monster behind him, just as they had suspected. He could almost feel Rob's breath on the back of his neck as he ran through the night.

The streetlights blinked wildly. The alarms of parked cars flared in unison. The lights behind him were dying, leaving the streets in shadows. Kevin yelled at the top of his lungs for help as his legs began to surrender, slowing down. A pain in his side forced him to lay his hand on his rib. The putrid scent of burned flesh filled his nose.

He was going to die, he was sure of that. It was only a matter of time. Sirens echoed in the distance, and a glimmer of hope grew inside him. He crossed the street at full speed toward his only chance of salvation.

A police car skidded in front of him. Kevin hit the hood of the car and was propelled back, hitting the pavement. He raised his hands in the air as he struggled to his feet. Two cops stepped out of the car in bewilderment, both carrying their pistols and pointing at him. Kevin looked down, realizing that he was covered with glass and blood that wasn't his. Their faces paled at the sight.

"No! Please!" Kevin yelled. "You don't understand! Somebody's chasing me!"

They both opened fire, and Kevin closed his eyes. He could feel the scrape of bullets flying beside him. He waited for a stabbing pain that would knock him to the pavement, but it never came.

"Behind you!" yelled one of the officers.

Kevin opened his eyes, realizing that they were not shooting at him. He ran towards the car as the cops shot at the beast behind him. Rob jumped into the hood of the car and climbed up to the roof. One of Rob's spider legs pierced through the officer's chest and emerged from his back. Kevin threw himself to the other side of the car, hitting the ground and looking up. Rob jumped on the second officer who was still frantically firing a pistol that had already run out of bullets. Rob stuck an appendage in the officer's eye while the other separated the head from his body with a quick and clean cut.

Kevin got into the driver's seat of the squad car and closed the door. He turned the keys still hanging from the steering wheel. The car roared. Kevin took one last look before stepping on the pedal with all his strength. The fire that had once enveloped Rob was gone; what remained was melting skin, exposing his muscles and burned veins. Half his face was a liquefied mixture of black, red and pink.

Kevin floored the gas pedal and looked in the rearview mirror. Rob was running towards him at an impressive speed, almost catching up to the car. Kevin sighed with relief once he noticed that the monster was falling behind.

He meditated for a second on where he should go and concluded that his best bet was the police station. It wasn't the safest place in the world, but if Cleyton wasn't there, then he'd be surrounded by a group of armed men in case something went wrong. Besides, he would have a chance to meet up with James.

CHAPTER 29

Lia pulled her sister through a dark alley, looking over her shoulder to make sure no one was following them. Once they were certain that they were alone, the sisters slowed down to a halt. Sofia rested against the wall, panting as hard as her sister. Both were drenched in sweat. Lia felt like she had run for hundreds of miles, but even though that wasn't the case, they'd gone quite far. Fear was a good incentive for cardio.

"What was that? That was not a human being," said Lia, catching her breath.

"I have no idea," said Sofia. "Kevin is the one who usually has an answer for everything, and I think even he doesn't know."

"He killed Mom, Sofi..." Lia put both hands on her face and started sobbing. "He killed Mom, and I don't know where Dad is."

Sofia succumbed to the piercing pain in her heart and cried with her sister. She slid down to the floor, put her knees to her chest and let herself go. Lia sat down beside her and put her arm around Sofia. They both stayed there, without moving, without saying a word. It wasn't until Sofia got a hold of the situation they were in that she shouted, "Kevin, we have to help him!"

"H-how?" Lia asked as she wiped the tears from her face, which was red and swollen. She was still breathless. "We can't go back... don't make me go back..."

"That would be suicide. At least that's what Kevin would say." She shook her head. "I don't know, I don't know what to do."

"What would he do?"

"Kevin? I'm not sure. Something smart."

"Like what?"

"Go somewhere safe, a place where those monsters can't find us, and look for help. I think the police station is our best choice. Somebody there could help us."

Sofia stood up with difficulty, offering her hand to Lia, who accepted. Holding hands, they resumed making their way to the station. Once they reached the avenue, Lia looked up at a column of smoke rising in the distance coming from their neighborhood.

"Is that our house?" Lia asked.

"Probably." Sofia's voice was a barely-audible whisper.

Lia tried to erase that image from her mind. There had been enough tragedies for one night to add to the fact that they might've been left homeless, and even if they were, that was the least of their worries now. They continued walking, now hugging each other to fight the cold. A cloud of vapor escaped their lips with each breath, and little snowflakes started dancing in the beams of the streetlights. The first snow of winter had come at the worst possible moment.

In the distance, several rumbles echoed through the night. They were gunshots. Sofia shuddered at what that might mean. Several police sirens screamed in unison, flooding the streets with red and blue lights. Lia let go of her sister and ran to the middle of the road as if a suicidal demon had possessed her. Sofia ran after her to make sure she didn't get hurt. They both were on the verge of madness. It wasn't just the monsters in the dark, but these overwhelming emotions that made the present situation dangerous.

A black Ford crossed the street at an ungodly speed. The tires squealed, raising smoke when taking the curve. The car came closer and closer to the disoriented and disconsolate girl who was in the middle of the street, waving her arms in the air, begging for help.

"Look out!" Sofia yelled at her sister.

Sofia jumped towards Lia and tackled her to the ground. The car flew past them, a few feet away from running them over.

"What the hell?" Lia moaned. Her eyes were wide open, and her face had paled to match the snow. "What's wrong with that guy?"

"What did you expect? You were in the middle of the street!" Sofia yelled, standing up and brushing the dirt off her pants.

"I'm sure he was drunk," Lia concluded as she got up.

Not long after, the black car crashed into a tree. The impact lifted the back of the car off the ground for a second. A few branches fell on top of it. A man covered from head to toe with blood blew out of the windshield from the driver's seat. Lia covered her mouth with her hand to drown a scream. The man collapsed facedown on a sea of broken glass.

The sisters looked around, trying to see if somebody else had witnessed the accident and would offer their help. They were the only ones present. Lia took a step forward and then back, doubtful. Sofia nodded at her and headed towards the wounded man. Lia followed. The closer she got, the more her urges to vomit increased. She was sure she had seen more blood that night than most people had in a lifetime.

A crisp sound alerted them as they approached the body covered in red. It was as if the man's bones had made their way through his organs. His back had four lumps that seemed about to burst. The girls backed away slowly.

The tumors on the man's back finally exploded, revealing what appeared to be needle-like bones moving erratically and unnaturally. They looked like the legs of an insect turned on his back, trying to make sense of the world around it. The dead man's head twisted backward, looking straight at them. A movement that would break a normal person's spine.

The girls screamed and rushed as fast as they could in the opposite direction before the man could get up. They ran for what seemed like a thousand miles until they reached the center of the town. The police sirens were still ringing, louder and louder as they got closer to the source of the sound. More shots. The smell of burning wood filled their lungs. Sofia looked up at the sky; there were several black columns coming from a bunch of different places.

The sisters were in the middle of the commercial area where the locals used to shop, the youngsters would go out on weekends to hang out or, after a long day at work, people would buy candy for their children at home.

Now everything was in ruins. It seemed like a hurricane had devastated the place. Most of the store windows were broken. There was a car upside down in the middle of the street, and one of the residential buildings spat fire out of every window. They saw figures passing by them, shadows of people whose faces reflected confusion and horror.

"W-what's going on?" Lia asked, looking around her. Time slowed down almost to a halt. Every second stretched out, and every detail of that misery pulsed in her heart.

Amidst the multitude of frightened shadows came a woman, carrying her son in her arms. He could be no more than five. His blond curls contrasted with red from a wound on his forehead. The woman pleaded for help, shouting that they had killed her husband and taken their other child.

"We are not the only ones," Sofia whispered in shock.

The next thing that happened confirmed her suspicions. A humanoid creature about seven feet tall with black eyes, shark-like teeth, and claws as long as butcher knives jumped out of the darkness, tearing a man in half like paper. The man's last cries of pain were overshadowed by those of the people around him. Lia and Sofia stood paralyzed. Neither knew where to run now. Lia's legs wouldn't hold her for long.

"Come on, we have to go!" Sofia cried, seeing her sister's catatonic face.

Lia obeyed. At that moment, anyone could have told her to jump off a bridge, and she would do so without hesitation. She had lost any notion of where they were going or what they were doing there in the first place. Then, Sofia remembered what they had discussed in the alleyway. The police station was only a couple of blocks away.

A blanket of darkness covered the road. The lights of the town had disappeared by sectors, and the one they were in had already gone dark. Not even the moon was present to guide those lost souls in the night. The only thing they could count on was the faint orange glow coming from the fires all over town. Lia felt as if her lungs wouldn't last much longer. Sofia seemed to be just like her, and their sprint turned to a light jog.

Sofia let out a shriek of happiness when she saw the sign reading *Heaven's Peak Police Department*. However, Lia noticed that there weren't any police cars in the parking lot, just a few unmarked cars. They both slowed down as they approached. Something wasn't right. That thought crossed both of their minds, and the girls exchanged glances.

"Maybe they're out there trying to help people. The town is falling apart," Lia suggested with a hint of hope.

"Everybody at the same time," said Sofia in a pessimistic tone.

They decided to go around the parking lot to look in through the windows. They were now using darkness in their favor. From where they were, they could see clearly inside the station.

At the reception desk, there was a woman in a green suit with the phone still in her hand. What was left of her head was a mass of brains, bits of hair, and fragments of bones that decorated the wall behind her. Sofia put a hand on her mouth to stifle a scream. Lia, for her part, was bowled over. All of a sudden, a man in a gray suit came out of one of the reception doors, running with his hand covering his bloodstained arm. Sofia squinted, not believing what she was seeing. Agent Norman James took one last look over his shoulder before sprinting into the parking lot, directly to the black car. Sofia stood up and opened her mouth to call out for him, but Lia grabbed her arm and pointed at the entrance again. Another man appeared, with a gray beard. His face seemed to have open wounds that pierced his face like veins, and his eyes dark like coal. Sofia ducked again. Lia led her to some bushes near them. They remained crouched, expectantly, trying not to make any noise as they watched James get into his car. Lia squeezed Sofia's arm, digging her nails into her sister's skin as she watched a humanoid monster leap over James's car. Another landed on the roof. The agent opened fire on the creature and stepped on the accelerator. His car brushed against the walls of the parking lot, sparking before he sped off into the street, taking the monsters with him.

At the front door, the man with the beard swept his dark gaze around. The girls lowered their heads until they were almost kissing the ground. Finally, the man got into another car and left, leaving the parking lot empty except for them. The girls waited until there was no sign of anyone before breathing normally again.

"We have to go in," said Lia.

"Did you lose your mind?" Sofia asked. "Didn't you see that? That man covered in blood was our only hope."

"And the station is empty."

"We don't know that. What if everyone inside is dead or possessed?"

"There's no safe place left in this town, Sofie, not tonight. But, perhaps, not everything is lost."

"What are you talking about?" Sofia was beginning to feel like the last sane person in the world.

"Think about it. They probably have somebody's phone number from outside Heaven's Peak. If we could contact the police from a neighboring town, they could come and help. News would travel fast."

Sofia sighed, closing her eyes. Lia could tell her sister didn't like the idea in the slightest, but if there was a possibility, no matter how small, that they could get help, they had to try. Besides, they didn't have much left to lose. Lia grabbed her hand, entwining her fingers with Sofia's.

"The nearest town is miles away. It'll take forever for them to arrive," Sofia pointed out.

"It's our only chance."

They got up and took a quick look around, crossing the parking lot with their heads low. They reached the main entrance and opened the double glass doors with extreme care as if a single blow could knock it down. All they could hear was the roar of the wind against the windows. The girls entered, covering their mouths and trying to ignore the receptionist's decapitated corpse.

They made their way to the cubicles, looking with keen eyes for some paper stuck on the wall. They were expecting red letters and arrows pointing to the phone number of another police department but instead found a massacre.

There must've been at least half a dozen officers, all inert on the floor, in puddles of their own blood and dismembered parts. Lia squeezed her sister's hand, shaking and sweating.

Sofia pulled her sister to the office corridor, doing her best not to look around. She could feel a tickling sensation running through her body as if thousands of ants marched beneath her skin. When they arrived, she glanced over the names on each door until she found the sheriff's office. If anyone had a way to contact the other police departments, it was him. Lia stood next to her sister, shoulder-to-shoulder, in front of the door, doubtful about how to proceed.

Sofia gently pushed the door. Her heart skipped a beat as Sheriff Thomas Gordon gave her an inert look, his body tilted to the side of the chair. His chest had been blown wide open, exposing his guts, and blood dripped all over his clothes and desk. Lia brought her fingers to the roots of her hair and squeezed so hard it seemed she was about to rip them out. Sofia put her hands on her sister's shoulders and looked into her eyes, which were ready to burst into tears again.

"Calm down, calm down," Sofia said.

"I can't. I can't go on like this." Lia fell to her knees. Sofia knelt in front of her, making sure she didn't look into the office.

"We have a plan, okay? And we're going to stick with it no matter what happens. It's our only hope, you said it yourself."

Sofia put her arms around Lia and let her sob. She had the urge to burst into tears as well, but she resisted. One of them had to be strong.

If they both fell into despair, they wouldn't make it. Again, she thought about Kevin and how he would act in this situation.

"I'll go in alone and look for the phone number. You stay here and watch my back," Sofia said.

"No, please, stay with me," Lia pleaded.

"Together, then."

Sofia got up, held out her hand to Lia, and led her toward the office. They approached the desk, covering their noses with their blouses to avoid the smell of death. They searched the desk drawers without finding anything but documents and useless memos. The sheriff's body covered the last remaining drawer. Lia cast an inquiring glance at Sofia, and she understood. Each of them grabbed an arm of the chair, doing their best not to touch the sheriff, and pushed. The chair barely rolled a few inches. She took a deep breath and gave one last push that knocked the corpse to the ground. The girls squealed at the hollow bang.

Gordon's gaze now looked toward the ceiling, immutable. Lia crouched down, and searched the drawer quickly, trying to get it over with.

"I think I found it," said Lia.

"Let me see," said Sofia without believing her ears. Lia gave her the paper, and she examined it. "This is just a letter from the sheriff, Lia, what are you talking about?"

"Look at where it's from. Brian Morris, the lieutenant in the police department in the other county. Looks like they know each other."

"You're right, Lia. Oh, my God." Sofia examined the letter and confirmed what her sister was saying. Indeed the letter came from there, and it showed a telephone number to contact him.

Sofia went to grab the white telephone on the edge of the desk. Red spots stood out from the gleaming white. She grabbed it with her thumb and index finger and began to dial. She put the phone within inches of her ear until she heard it ring. Lia stood beside her, expectant. Their hearts flipped as they listened to a male voice on the other side of the line.

"Lieutenant Brian Morris, how can I help you?"

"L-lieutenant, we're calling you from Heaven's Peak police department. The whole town has gone mad! You have to send someone!"

"H-hello? If this is some kinda joke—"

"No, it's not! I swear!"

The lieutenant took a couple of seconds to say something again.

"Please, identify yourself."

"M-my name is Sofia Everett. I came to the police station thinking it was safe but everybody here is dead! Please, we need help!"

"Miss, stay calm. Please, tell me, where's Sheriff Thomas Gordon?"

"He's dead!" Sofia was starting to sweat.

"What do you mean, he's dead?"

"Somebody killed him! I'm looking at his corpse right now!"

"Do you know who killed him?" the lieutenant asked. He was starting to show more interest, but his cold demeanor remained; that only made her more nervous.

"No! The whole town is dead! It's a massacre! Please, you have to send someone now!"

"Don't worry, miss. Stay put, we'll send reinforcements as soon as possible."

Sofia and Lia exchanged hopeful glances and squeezed each other's hands.

"Oh, my God, yes, thank you. When will you be here?"

"There's a snowstorm tonight so you'll have to stay where you are. Reinforcements will arrive at dawn."

"What?" Sofia and Lia yelled in unison.

"That's too long!" Sofia cried. "We don't have that much time!"

"I'm very sorry. What I recommend is that you look for a safe place and stay there for a few hours until we arrive."

The lights flickered, and a dial tone came from the phone. The call had been cut off.

"Hello? Hello!" Sofia shouted, clutching the phone to her ear. "Damn it!"

She threw the phone against the table. Her worst fear had become a reality. They were trapped there, forced to stay put for who knows how long while the storm passed. There were still hours left until dawn. Bringing people from another county up there in the dark and snow would be a disaster. They had no choice but wait. She looked at Lia, who seemed to have aged about ten years in just a couple of hours.

They left the office, afraid that the possessed cop from earlier could jump out of any corner. Once in the hall, they looked at the nameplates on each door once again to guide themselves. Norman James's office door was wide open, with a gaping hole in the center. They decided it wasn't the best place to spend the night, so they went into a random office and locked the door.

Sofia turned off the lights and sat in the dark with her sister. It didn't take long before her eyes became accustomed to the gloom, and the light of the street offered them a little more visibility. The area they were in was like the last candle on a cake that refused to go out.

Sofia knew that the window in front of them should show a beautiful landscape, but the mountains were indistinguishable from the black sky. That was until she saw a red glow jumping from the ground, daring to touch the heavens. It was a flare coming from the woods. It was Kevin, it had to be. She knew it was him. However, she didn't know that it would be the last she ever saw of him.

CHAPTER 30

❧

"All units! I want you to keep an eye on all the exits of Heaven's Peak as well as the main and west avenues! Your priority is to find Agent Norman James! I want every available officer on his ass! Look in every corner! A snowstorm is coming, so he won't get far! He's the one you can thank for all this mayhem!"

It was Lieutenant Spencer Cleyton's voice coming from the squad car's radio. Kevin had to make a conscious effort not to crash after listening to such bullshit.

How the fuck could they have come up with that? he wondered.

His surprise and confusion turned into fear at the thought of the agent's situation. It was no accident. It was no coincidence. Someone in the police department had incriminated him for getting too close to the truth. Kevin struck the wheel in frustration and felt his heart quicken as he succumbed to anger, fear, and helplessness.

A car sped by, and for a fraction of a second Kevin saw its occupants. It was a family of five: a man at the wheel covered in red, his face a reflection of sheer horror, his wife unconscious (or dead) in the passenger seat, and three children in the rear seats crying their hearts out.

Kevin stepped on the gas as he passed houses drowned in darkness, some intact, others with broken windows and corpses in the courtyards like creepy Halloween decorations. Snowflakes danced in front of the headlights, and he could swear that there was more snow with each passing second. Though the car windows were closed, the cold crept in from somewhere, making his fingers barely able to move. Little clouds began to exhaled out of his nose.

Outside, the snow mixed with the ash coming from the columns of smoke rising all over Heaven's Peak.

Kevin gripped the wheel tightly as he figured out where to go now. The police station was out of the question, and there were officers at every town exit. He had no safe place to retreat to. Besides, he still had no idea of James' whereabouts. The only thing that relieved him was that, apparently, they hadn't been able to find James. The agent must be hiding somewhere; the question was where.

Kevin slammed on the brakes as he saw a humanoid creature cross the road right in front of him. The car skidded from one side to the other, trying to obey the direction in which the steering wheel moved. The car flew to the side of the road, heading straight for the trees, the tires struggled against the stones until he crashed into a pine at the passenger's seat. Kevin staggered from side to side, held in place by his seatbelt. Broken glass flew in all directions, and his head bounced against the steering wheel. The beacon lights flickered and disappeared completely as the snow fell gently on the roof of the shattered police car.

Kevin grunted as he opened his eyes. His hand moved across the seat until he found the seatbelt buckle. He unbuckled it and opened the door. His body surrendered as he stepped out of the car and fell flat on the ground. He put both hands on the cold lawn and struggled to get on his feet, staggering back toward the road. He held his left arm over his ribs, which throbbed with pain; he was sure something was broken. He used his right hand to grope in the dark and find support in the trees around him.

He had barely reached the side of the road when he slumped on his back to sit down. A chilly breeze shook the bare branches of the trees. In the distance, he could hear screams, sirens, and gunshots. Kevin sighed, as deeply as he could. There was no escape. The road he was on led to the outskirts of town. If he decided to go that route, sooner or later he would meet a bunch of trigger-happy cops waiting for him, anxious to put a bullet into anything that moved. He could follow the road through the woods, but if the police didn't catch him, the monsters surely would. Even if he survived all of that, the storm was only going to get worse.

He thought about Sofia and everything she was going through. Just like him, she had lost a sibling and both parents. Unlike him though, she didn't have the time to mourn them. She had witnessed horrible and traumatic events, and she still had to stay strong for her sister. At that moment, Kevin felt a sense of admiration for her. She must be so scared, confused and broken. He couldn't let anything happen to her, even if that meant the unthinkable. Not too long ago, Kevin was more than willing to give his life to save his sister, but right there and then, with everything that had been going on, he didn't know if that was even possible. Even if he managed to find her, she would probably be dead already. Kevin felt a stab in his chest as the thought crossed his mind. That was the hard truth, and he had to accept it. Sofia, however, was still alive, so he had to focus all of his efforts to keep it that way. He put a hand on his pocket and felt the shape of the flare gun on his side.

He paid attention to his surroundings. He could hear the water crashing against rocks nearby, which meant he was close to the river. That was his only clue to his whereabouts, and he decided to follow it. He walked for a while, guided by the sound of running water. Once he realized that he'd finally reached the river, he took a couple of steps back to avoid falling into it by accident.

Kevin took a long, deep breath. He knew that if he went in the opposite direction of the current, he would get to the mines. He knew that Sofia was out there, scared, trying to make sense of an impossible situation. He knew that Jenny was still out there, probably in the mines, alive or dead, and he had to see her one last time. There was only one thing left to do. He remembered the night he'd locked himself in the motel's restroom and what he'd thought when he held those pills in his hand. He wondered if what he was about to do wasn't the equivalent of that.

He reached into his pocket again and pulled out the flare gun. He caressed it, pondering whether he was doing the right thing or if he was just being guided by desperation. There were only two more flares left. Fuck it. If he managed to focus all of the chaos on him instead of Sofia and everybody else, then it was something he had to do.

"Try and find me, motherfuckers," he said, raising the gun to the night sky.

Kevin pulled the trigger. A blinding light jumped out of the gun and painted the mountains red.

CHAPTER 31

Norman James saw it, along with several dozen people scattered around the town: a crimson flame that split the sky in half. It was a desperate scream for help in that night's darkest hour. James felt goose bumps run down his back.

He had been inspecting the wound on his shoulder before turning his attention to the sky, parked on the side of the road. His mind was still trying to process what was happening. In less than a few hours, the entire town had fallen into total chaos. Men, women, and children were attacking each other while inhuman creatures lurked the streets.

It was too much. It went against everything he ever thought possible. James had been raised in a Christian family. His mother was loving, although a bit superstitious. His father was cold-minded and calculating; the kind of personality expected from a detective.

Every night, his mother would pray for her husband to get back home safely from work, a job which according to her was very dangerous.

Someday you'll get to my doorstep with a bullet in your gut, she used to say.

James had grown up to be like his father. Always questioning everything, never taking anything for granted, and always searching for the truth. Little Norman used to wonder if his mother's prayers really worked. After all, his father never got badly hurt and lived well past his seventies. A veteran, no doubt.

At that moment, the agent felt like a kid again. He wondered if asking for mercy from a being that never replied could ever work.

James closed his eyes and prayed.

Once he finished mentally reciting all the prayers he remembered, he fixed his eyes on the steering wheel, where he had left bloody red handprints. Going back to the hotel room where he was staying was out of the question. He was sure they would be waiting for him there. They would be waiting for him anywhere, actually. There was no safe place in this godforsaken town.

He looked up. The red light had created a bright arc in the dark sky as it fell. He was sure it came from deep in the forest and wondered who would be so stupid to think that that would help them in such a situation. It would only attract the attention of every bloodthirsty creature and wacko in the area. Then he understood. It wasn't a cry for help, it was a taunt. *Find me if you can,* said the flare in the sky.

It was just a guess, but he had nowhere else to go. Besides, even in the dark of night, he knew that the flare came from somewhere near the mines. He remembered the pictures Kevin had left on his desk along with the note. The only person apart from him who knew what was in the mines was Kevin, but the chances of that being him were minimal, considering that he would have to have survived for that long.

In the worst-case scenario, he would find somebody alone and disoriented in the middle of the forest. He didn't give it much more thought. As if possessed by an outside force, he stepped on the gas and took the road heading towards the flare. The flame was slowly fading.

He turned in a tight curve, trying not to lose control of the car. The road was already slippery. The engine roared with impetus as it accelerated. He crossed to the next bend and noticed that he was moving away from the flash. It came from the woods, so the only way he could get to it was on foot. He parked the car as close as he could, pulled a flashlight out of the glove compartment, and hurried off.

James ran as far as he could through the deserted woods. The faint red dazzle had almost disappeared, but he didn't need it to guide himself. He was definitely going up the river toward the abandoned mines.

As he dodged the branches of the trees and puddles that were starting to freeze, he heard them: creatures of the night, moving through the forest. The branches breaking, and the crunching of the earth by dozens of supernatural footsteps. His heart started pounding. He felt dozens of shadows passing by his side, indifferent to his presence as if he were invisible.

The light from his torch reflected on the ground, and James suddenly stopped when he realized he had found a river. He lifted the lantern above him and saw the creatures contorting their bodies in ways that made it possible to cross from branch to branch, clinging to them with claws as long as butcher knives. There were three of them, hurriedly going in the opposite direction of the stream.

With his heart in his throat, uncertain of his own mental state, James decided to follow them, pointing the light at the ground to avoid accidentally stumbling into the frozen water. He had to raise his knees almost to his chest while climbing up the hill. A white mantle of snow already obscured the earth. Supernatural grunts came from the branches above him.

Once he reached a clearing, he saw a massive rectangular structure at the foot of the mountain, barely visible, camouflaged in shades of black. He didn't have to be a genius to figure out where he was. James ran to the mouth of the mountain. He didn't see the person who fired the flare. He wasn't even sure if that person was still alive.

His mind strayed from that thought. Now he faced another opportunity. He would find out once and for all what was going on in that cursed town. The agent stepped into the dark tunnel as his flashlight began to blink.

The battery was taking its last breath.

CHAPTER 32

The only thing around him was darkness so dense he could almost feel it, like a mist in which the cold penetrated the bones and shook them. Kevin's senses sharpened, his wet clothes squeezing his skin, embracing him. His ear could catch the most distant drops of water falling from some rusty pipe. Except something was different, he couldn't figure out exactly what, but something was missing.

Silence. The place was completely quiet except for the leaks. Last time he was here, a humming sound made its way around the site as if a giant monster had been sleeping deep inside the mines. Where was the buzzing caused by the ventilation system?

His nose caught mixed wet and putrid smells; rusty metal, dead animals and dirt that had never seen the light of day.

With beads of cold sweat running down his back, he crept through the tunnel, trying to guess his position. Kevin raised his hands, unable to even see them. He blinked several times to make sure his eyes were open; they were, but it didn't make a difference. That was until he saw a column of light behind him. It seemed to come from a flashlight. He could scarcely distinguish the silhouette of the person who carried it: a tall, slender figure staggering along. He was sure that it was male. For a moment, he felt certain that it was the agent, but the rational side of his mind told him that was too good to be true. His mind was trying to give him hope in a moment when there wasn't any. He decided against testing his luck and got as far away as he could from that light, which began to blink sporadically until it disappeared altogether.

He seized the opportunity, put his hand against the wall and guided himself in the opposite direction. His walk became a sprint as he heard the footsteps behind him. He reached into the pocket of his jacket. Only one flare left. Having the gun between his fingers made him feel safer, he pulled it out for a fraction of a second just to put it back. He was only going to use it if it was absolutely necessary.

Kevin stopped short as his hand met the corner of the wall. He felt the sudden urge to scream at the top of his lungs and demand to know who was out there, but he stopped the words from leaving his mouth. He gripped the flare gun with both hands and moved to the side.

His eyes were struggling to adjust; however, he did manage to distinguish a couple of silhouettes, some darker than others. Some were rectangular, metal boxes; others cylindrical, probably containers of some sort. He started running and stumbled, trying to dodge the obstacles and dumping several barrels in his path. Adrenaline rushed through his veins, his body was no longer his own, possessed by a pure, primal instinct for survival. His fingers glided across the wall until he felt cold, rusted steel in his quivering hands. He reached for the handle and turned it as he put all his weight against the door to slam it open and shut it behind him. On the other side, he could hear the man's steps.

Yet another sound made his blood run cold. It was a strange mixture between the howl of a dying animal and a human cry. It came from within the mines.

CHAPTER 33

⤴

Norman James was sure he'd heard someone the moment his flashlight went off. He stood there, paralyzed and unsure of how to proceed. He couldn't see a damn thing and whoever was in the darkness with him had the upper hand. Then there was the noise, a thundering blow of metal that echoed through the tunnel and pierced his ears. Then another one. In a matter of seconds, all James could hear was a cacophony of clashing metal, as if whoever was in front of him had gone apeshit. No, it was more like they were running away. James blindly followed the sound, almost tripping on the barrels that rolled over the ground. He raised his hands and felt the cold surface of the rusty metal door in front of him. Whoever was in the dark with him a couple of seconds ago had gone through there. He took out his revolver and held it tight as he stepped inside. A loud, animal-like cry echoed from that direction.

James felt all the hairs on his body standing on end. He expected someone to jump out from the shadows, but nobody did. He waited a couple of minutes, convinced that his vision would adjust sooner or later. Realizing that such a thing would not happen, he felt the pockets of his suit, praying to find something to shed some light. A lighter would've been useful, but it had been years since he'd smoked. He could imagine the faint flame rippling from side to side, dancing to the beat of some inaudible music. But no, instead, he had a good-for-nothing flashlight with no batteries, and now he had to find his way around by dragging his feet and raising his hands like a monkey in a circus. He walked a couple of feet before the tip of his toe kicked something on the floor. It sounded like it was rolling. He heard screeching metal against the dirt.

Could it be? he wondered.

James crouched and picked up the cylindrical object. It was, it definitely was, and he couldn't believe his luck. Another flashlight. He looked for the on button with his thumb. If it worked then that could lead to two different scenarios. One, he would finally be able to see his surroundings and begin his search; the other, that he would be surrounded by the demonic creatures, and the light would reveal his exact position to them.

It's worth it, he thought. *Beats having to walk through the dark.*

James pushed the button, and a column of light shot out. The agent moved the bright circle around him. He was inside a vast structure whose ceiling was almost invisible, with metal fences that separated the place into sections. He looked up and saw a huge fan, motionless. However, unlike everything else around him, there was no sign of decay or even spider webs around it. Could it be that it was working until recently? If that was the case...

"Son of a bitch."

He squeezed his revolver tightly to keep it from slipping through his sweaty hands. He gasped with difficulty as his brain was still trying to process what had happened. Ironically, he felt calmer, perhaps because he could see where he was now.

He backed away slowly until he was against the wall, holding his revolver high and sliding his way through with all his senses alert, attentive to any movement. A hard bump startled him. He turned and aimed his weapon at the source of the sound.

A figure stood near a few barrels, but it wasn't what he expected. It had no extra legs or tentacles coming out of its back. It was a simple humanoid silhouette. The dim light barely let him distinguish the face of the person, who had raised their hands in the air as a sign of surrender. James narrowed his eyes to make sure that what he was seeing was real.

Kevin Miller lowered one of his hands to his face and placed his index finger to his lips. James nodded, and slowly aimed his gun at the ground. He glanced around, making sure there was no one watching them from the shadows. The agent approached the boy, stretched out his arms and wrapped them tightly around him. He found himself surprised at his own reaction. He'd never been the emotional type so he couldn't imagine just how confused the boy must have been to find a person he'd only seen a couple of times and give him a hug. It wasn't as if they'd known each other for that long.

"I knew it was you!" James exclaimed, pulling away from him. "The flare. I knew it had to be you. Even though I thought you were dead."

"You thought I was dead?" Kevin asked. "Well, I don't blame you, but then why did you come here?"

James didn't know how to answer. "I guess I had nothing else to lose."

Kevin looked down and pointed to the agent's revolver. "That's not going to work."

"I know, but it makes me feel safe."

"This may be better." Kevin pulled out the flare gun and showed it to the agent.

James frowned. "That's better than a revolver?"

"Yes. The skin of those monsters is hard as steel, but it can be burned. That's how I survived."

"The fires," James muttered.

"What?"

"The fires all over town. These things are attacking everyone, so you probably weren't the only one to discover their weakness."

"I guess," Kevin replied with a shrug. "I only have one left, so it's not like I have many options."

"The only option we have left is to keep going. There's nothing left to lose. What the fuck are those things anyway?"

"It has something to do with that black goo. It's like a disease that makes people go crazy and violent." Kevin stopped talking before saying too much. He had been infected too, and he didn't know how much time he had before the symptoms started showing. He wanted to tell James, but he kept his mouth shut, refusing to acknowledge the fact that he didn't have much time left, as if that would make it untrue.

"A disease?" James asked. "No, it's different. It's more like they're possessed. God, I sound so crazy right now."

"What do you mean possessed?"

"Cleyton, the Lieutenant. That guy was an asshole, but he was no murderer. I mean, at first, I thought the police were corrupt, and they were sweeping everything under the rug. Now, I think it's because they were afraid. They didn't know what they were gonna find and they didn't want to." James took a deep breath. "Anyway, I'm babbling too much. The point is that Cleyton may have been crooked, but he was not a killer. Not too long ago a suspect spat something on him, a black goo like you call it, and ever since then, he started acting differently. Things escalated and, well, he slaughtered the only people left in the police department."

"So you think he got infected and that's why he killed them?"

"That's what I'm trying to say. He seemed lucid. Like he knew what he was doing. He may just have gone mad but, I don't know, there was something in his voice, like something controlling him. Fuck, I sound like a superstitious idiot."

"You're not. I know what you mean. We need to get to the bottom of this."

"We will."

Kevin nodded. James caught something in the young man's eyes that shocked him. Anyone else in a similar situation would've been resigned to their fate and accepted their death, or denied it in a futile attempt to deal with something so unavoidable and out of their control. However, what he saw in the boy's eyes was an unshakable determination, like someone who would go to hell and back if necessary. At that moment, James felt a great deal of respect for him. Maybe in the future, once he was old enough and had the right training, he could be part of the FBI. That is if they managed to get out alive, of course. James smiled at the idea of having a pupil. After what happened to his wife, he had never even considered the idea of having a child. The thought of being someone's mentor filled him with joy.

"Where did you find that?" Kevin asked, pointing at James' flashlight.

"On the ground a couple of minutes ago," James replied

"It's Sofia's," Kevin whispered. "From last time."

James raised the flashlight so he could see around him. He noticed that the boy was a mess. He had a wound on his forehead where blood was beginning to dry. His upper lip was split, and his hair was covered with dirt and snow. His shirt was stained with something dark and dried.

I hope its blood, James thought.

The agent kept his questions to himself. He could guess what had happened to him. Kevin pointed the flashlight into the hallway behind James.

"They came from there the last time I was here. This is as far as I've come."

"Then let's go deeper into the rabbit hole."

They continued down the tunnel, shoulder to shoulder. James tried to stay calm with breathing exercises. Inhale and exhale. Inhale and exhale. Slowly, again and again. However, each breath he took failed to fill his chest, as if his lungs had shrunk to the size of raisins. In a matter of seconds, the boy began to do the same thing, but every breath sounded like a snore.

"Be quiet," whispered James.

"I am."

"I can hear you breathing."

"I can hear you scolding me."

The agent didn't know how to respond to that. They reached what appeared to be a platform that served as an elevator. It had a panel in the center that dictated in which direction it would go. To his right, the smooth, firm walls turned into stone, and the padded floor became dirt and rock. It was the cave from which the raw material was extracted. While the elevator could take them to the points of interest quickly and practically, it would also alert whoever was in there of their presence. On the other hand, walking through the cave on foot meant taking the long way.

"I think it's pretty obvious where we should go," James said.

"Really? Because I have no idea what to do."

"The elevator is our safest option," said James. "Going through the cave would take us longer and who knows what we might find on the way. After all, this is their territory, not ours."

"But we could cover more ground through the cave. We also run the risk of the elevator leaving us right in front of an army of them."

James pondered his response. "Most of them are probably out there causing mayhem."

"Not after I put a huge red arrow over my head with a sign that said, 'Here I am,'" Kevin pointed out.

"Lower your voice," James ordered.

Kevin ran his hand over his head. He turned his back to James as he walked from one side to the other. "My sister could be out there, hidden, alone and scared."

"You should also consider the other possibility."

"If there's the slightest possibility that Jenny is alive, then I have to do everything I can to help her."

"And I understand, but I've been in this line of work long enough to know that, under these circumstances, a happy ending is very unlikely."

"I know," the boy 's voice broke, "but I still have to try."

Just as James was about to reply, a growl echoed in the darkness behind them, shaking the walls. James' first instinct was to point his revolver toward the source of the noise and repeatedly pull the trigger. Kevin threw himself into the elevator and activated the control panel, whose light went from red to green. Deafening outbursts rumbled in James' ears as Kevin called his name, begging him to get on the elevator before the platform began to descend, but the screams were dulled by a wave of grunts and shots.

In front of him, James could see human figures with masks running at full speed toward him and black-eyed monsters crawling on the ceiling like spiders. The officer glanced over his shoulder at the boy as the elevator pulled him down and out of view.

James felt his world fade before he realized that he had made the right decision. If those monsters had reached them, they both would have been lost, but now at least he could keep them at bay. Kevin had been able to escape, even though it was against his own will.

He kept pulling the trigger for a few seconds before realizing that there were no more bullets coming out. He felt the pockets of his suit and pants in a futile effort to find the ammo he knew he didn't have.

James dropped the revolver and closed his eyes.

CHAPTER 34

Kevin lost sight of the agent. The image of him shooting at the darkness was replaced by a stone wall as the elevator plunged downwards. Kevin screamed at the top of his lungs for James to come with him as tears slid from his face. The elevator shuddered under his feet, descending into the unknown.

"No, no, no, no, please."

Kevin pressed all the buttons on the console. No matter which buttons he pressed or how hard he pushed them, they wouldn't respond. The elevator continued to descend slowly but incessantly. The gunshots above him ceased, and Kevin felt his heart skip a beat. He had to go back.

He jerked the lever up and down several times and hit the panel so hard that his knuckles began to bleed. A massive sense of impotence filled every fiber of his being.

The metal under his feet stopped shaking. The elevator let out a metallic screech as it came to a full stop. In front of him was a cave supported by gears and metal tubes that stretched for miles, deep into the womb of the earth. The beams that rooted down the cave were rusted, seemingly about to fall apart.

Kevin hesitated as he set foot on the damp earth and felt the cold air hit his face. It was as if the mountain was alive and breathing, and he was digging straight into its belly, letting himself be devoured. He moved slowly through the entrails of the cave, putting one foot in front of the other only when he was sure that it was safe to walk on. The walls were getting closer.

The deeper he went, the more aware he became of the darkness hugging him from behind. He turned and pointed the flashlight back to see over his shoulder to make sure there was no monster breathing on his neck. There was nobody there, and for some reason, that made him even more worried.

He started walking faster, looking back sporadically. He stumbled repeatedly, and a few of those times he came close to slamming his face into the ground. He rested his hands on the stone walls in a futile attempt to keep them from getting closer. As the space shrank, his lungs protested with greater impetus. He was sweating buckets.

A cold breeze, another sigh from the mine, caressed his face once again. As he recovered his breath, he heard a purr in the distance. It was subtle —so much so that he had to pay attention to it, otherwise, it could've gone unnoticed— but it was undoubtedly there.

He walked to the source of the roar, unsure of what to expect. Eventually, he reached a stream of air coming from above. On top of him was a huge fan whose rusted blades were slowing down. It kept moving for several seconds before they stopped completely. Kevin remembered his last time in the mines, the man in the mask, Rob, had attacked him and broken one of the generators near the entrance. Apparently, it wasn't the only one, or this fan wouldn't have been working at all. Kevin wondered how many there were and what might've caused this one to stop. Maybe some fault in the electric current. After all, the place was really old and had been operating for a long time.

With a knot in his stomach, he continued his way through the cave until he saw a small hole at the end of the road. His heart skipped a beat once he saw that there might be a way out of this suffocating place. Luckily, the hole was wide enough to fit his body.

He went through headfirst with his arms reaching out, then his torso, and finally his legs. He fell on the rocky floor, shook the dust off his clothes as he stood up and raised the flashlight. He was in a much larger place; the light from his flashlight couldn't reach the ceiling. A black substance coated the walls, wrapping the whole area like a spider web. He could see bundles bound to the walls and scattered all over the cave, like Halloween decorations. It wasn't long before he realized they had the size and shape of human bodies. There were dozens, maybe hundreds.

Kevin felt lightheaded. His heart started racing, and nausea invaded his stomach. His mouth opened as he gagged. He managed to resist it at first, but it didn't take him long to fail. He stained the ground with that day's lunch, now processed in a confused mixture of juices. He closed his eyes and gagged again, this time nothing came out.

He wiped his lips with the sleeve of his jacket and rose to his feet. That black cobweb that enveloped the cave seemed to move, expanding and contracting as if it were breathing. He was trapped, swallowed by that beast that stretched for miles underground.

Once he gathered enough courage, Kevin advanced toward one of the bodies, flashlight high, guided by a morbid curiosity. Through the substance, he could see a pale, emaciated face that gave him an empty look. He lifted his hand, put one of his fingers in the viscous goo and pulled away as if it was hot. He rubbed his thumb with his index finger, it felt like glue.

Kevin took a closer look at the bodies one by one. Men, women, children, nobody had been spared. He knelt before one of the smaller corpses. The poor creature wrapped in the spider web didn't look older than eight, but there was something that set him apart from the rest. His face had more color than the others, and his blond hair was still radiant beneath the mucous blanket. To be sure, Kevin pressed his fingers to the boy's neck and waited. The boy had no pulse, but Kevin could tell from his appearance that it hadn't been very long.

Kevin drew closer, fearing that the boy would come out of his confinement and bite his face off. He looked familiar. It was then that Kevin realized who this boy was, and nausea threatened to seize him again. He had seen the boy in numerous missing person pamphlets all over town and in pictures decorating the walls in the Everett's house. It was Rudy.

He brought a fist to his mouth and bit it. He stood up and backed away slowly, feeling the blood leave his face. He looked around, desperate to find a way out. Sofia's brother had been missing for several weeks, he wasn't a coroner or anything like that, but the boy didn't seem to have been dead for more than a couple of days. His heart flipped at the thought that maybe, and just maybe, his sister might still be here, struggling to stay alive.

He reached into his jacket, pulled out the flare gun and aimed it at the ceiling. He could light up the whole place, and it would take the fraction of the time that he would need to illuminate each face with the flashlight. He put his finger on the trigger, and just as he was about to squeeze it, two images jumped out in his mind: The broken generator and the fan he saw turning off. If the ventilation system wasn't inactive before getting there, it was now. There was a chance that flammable gas had accumulated in the cave. He quickly lowered the pistol and put it back in his pocket, trembling and astonished at how close he had been to blowing everything up to pieces.

He sighed deeply. The only thing he could smell was putrefaction and death, no trace of gas. However, the most sensible thing would be to spare that last flare.

He had no choice but to aim the light of the flashlight at the corpses that hung from the walls and inspect them closely one by one. For Kevin, it felt like an eternity, but in reality, it hadn't been more than an hour. Every new dead face was a challenge to see. He couldn't help but imagine the story behind each and every one of them. A housewife who walked the neighborhood dogs last summer to make some extra cash to buy her children presents. The owner of a downtown business who, at seventy years of age, still made sure that everything in his shop was in place, and every customer was happy, always greeting them with a smile. And, just like Rudy, a child who thought it would be fun to play in the woods without supervision. They were all hanging on the wall now, inert.

He passed the flashlight over one of the bundles and recognized it instantly.

"Jenny."

It was her, no doubt. Kevin put the flashlight in his mouth, inserted both hands in the spider web and began to pull as best he could. It took a while, but he managed to get his sister's head out, one arm, then the other, the torso, and the legs last, her body falling on top of Kevin as he tried to catch her.

Tears streamed down his cheeks as he tore more pieces of spider web from Jenny's body. He reached out and held her in his arms. He didn't have to check her pulse. He could see her chest rise and fall, although her eyes were closed.

"Jenny! Come on, Jenny! Wake up!" Kevin yelled, shaking her.

There was no response; the girl was unconscious and didn't seem to have any intention of waking up. Kevin raised his hand and hesitated for a moment. He had to do it. He swung his palm with all of his strength, giving her a slap that turned her head to the side. Nothing.

"Dammit."

He fumbled for his flashlight and saw the column of light a few feet from him, pointing to one of the bundles, a small one. Rudy's innocent face gave him a cold, disapproving look. Kevin grabbed the flashlight and apologized to the little boy.

"I wish I had come sooner."

He carried his sister, stood up and looked at Rudy. He couldn't take them both. He couldn't help but feel great sorrow for Sofia, whom he had to tell what he'd seen. With Jenny in his arms, he went to the tunnel that seemed to be the only way out beside the hole he had gone through.

Kevin looked back one last time with tears in his eyes.

"I'm sorry."

CHAPTER 35

During what he thought would be his last breath, James' survival instinct kicked in. He opened his eyes to see a group of masked men with deformed appendages rushing toward him. Adrenaline ran through his body and propelled him into the tunnel to his left. Behind him, the elevator descended with the sixteen-year-old boy shouting his name. He jumped over a few rocks, dodging beams and pipes protruding from the walls.

He found several paths on the road, took one on the left, then followed another on the right. He had no idea where he was going. Every decision was made at the moment and at random, in an effort to make his pattern unpredictable. His lungs were burning. He tripped over a rock. His body fell to the side and rolled through a hole. His shoulder hit a metal beam and bounced against a wall before he hit the ground squarely.

He used his hands to push himself up and felt a hot fluid trickle down his nose. He brushed the blood off his face with his sleeve and looked up to see several shadows running where he had been a few seconds earlier. They hadn't seen him fall.

James turned off the flashlight and waited until he could hear nothing but silence. Once he was absolutely certain that there was nobody to worry about, he turned on the flashlight, put it in his mouth, and climbed on all fours up the hill and out of the hole with a few bruises. His best suit had turned to shit; he decided to head back the way he'd come.

As he walked along the rocky surface, his body complained more and more. Somehow, he managed to find the way back to the elevator. It was now just a hole in the darkness, surrounded by a metal railing with two buttons on a panel. He pressed one, but nothing happened. He continued exploring the place until he found a metal staircase that led to a booth.

He climbed up, trying to make as little noise as possible. From time to time he heard a growl in the distance that he couldn't identify.

What the fuck are those creatures? Am I supposed to believe they were humans once? Am I supposed to believe any of this?

His heart started beating faster the closer he got to the booth. At this point, anything could be behind that door. It was ajar, so he pushed it gently and peered in. The site was huge, with machines spread all over the place. James deduced that these were electric generators. He ran his hand over the cold metal and felt its purring. He circled the machine until he found a panel with buttons and a lever.

Not exactly sure what he was doing, but fully aware of what he wanted to accomplish, he pressed all the buttons he could and lowered the levers until the flickering lights went out. He repeated the process with the other machines until the only light source left was his flashlight. Oddly, one of the machine's panels seemed destroyed, smashed to pieces.

Probably the reason why there's no ventilation in this area.

James put a hand to his forehead and cleaned off the sweat with his sleeve. Within a couple of hours, the concentration of gases in the mine would grow to dangerous levels. Something as minimal as a spark could put him at risk. Until then, he had enough time to find Kevin and get out of there. He was aware that, in doing so, he would not find the answers he sought, but he was willing to accept that. He had to swallow his pride if he wanted to stop this madness once and for all.

A sharp knock behind him made him jump. Instinctively, he turned off the flashlight, bent down and put his back against the generator. He could barely make out an enormous shadow, almost seven feet high, hunched over with long claws. He stepped from one side to the other, trying to make as little noise as possible as he circled the machine. James could feel his heart beating all the way in his throat as he held his breath, afraid that even a small gasp would reveal his position. The creature got on all fours and circled the nearest generator, its claws scraping the ground.

James managed to grope the corner of the generator, taking a turn around it as the monster finished its round for the second generator. James crawled to the other side. The moment he reached the other generator, he put his arm on the ground, and his injured shoulder failed to hold his own weight. James slipped, and his head hit the metal, making a hollow echo that rang through the cave.

There was a spine-chilling roar, and the agent held his breath once again. The deformed shadow crossed from the corner straight to where he was. That was it. He was fucked.

James closed his eyes as the creature approached, waiting for its sharp teeth to gnaw on his face. The screeching sound of claws scraping the floor stopped. James could feel hot air, a putrid smell coming out the creature's jaws, hit his face. Slowly, the agent opened his eyes. The monster was a few inches from his face, its white fangs glittering in the darkness.

James had thought that these beasts could see in the dark. Yet, here he was, prey sitting right in front of his predator, and it hadn't attacked. His fall from earlier had drenched him in mud, so perhaps his scent was masked. It was a matter of time before the creature noticed his presence, so he decided to take a risk against his own judgment.

He slowly pulled the revolver from his holster. The monster grunted. James held in a scream. He raised his hand high and threw the weapon as far as he could.

The gun bounced against a generator all the way to the other side of the room. The metallic clash alerted the beast, which shrieked and then jumped in that direction. James lunged toward the exit. He shoved the door open and closed it behind him as he went down the stairs, trying his best not to stumble.

Once he reached the last step, he ran to the hole where the elevator used to be and leaned over the metal rods that surrounded it. He turned on the flashlight and pointed it down. The light dissipated in the darkness below. James thought he'd done what was best, risking his own life to keep Kevin safe, but now he realized that most likely he'd only put the boy in greater danger. He had managed to outsmart the masked group and make them go in another direction, but he didn't know the mines. He might have actually led them straight to Kevin's location by accident. Also, turning off the electricity right after the boy went through the elevator wasn't his best idea either.

It was only a matter of time before the toxic, and highly flammable gases filled every corner of the mines, in which case, two things could happen: they would suffocate by breathing in the poisoned air, or a spark somewhere would turn them all into a cloud of dust.

He looked down, crouched almost to the point of kissing the ground, and watched. There were traces of footsteps mixed with each other, painting a confused play but clearly showing where the person who'd left them had gone. He stood and glimpsed the dark tunnel in front of him.

With a deep sigh, he set himself a new goal: find Kevin Miller and get him out of there.

CHAPTER 36

Kevin's arms were worn out from the effort of holding his sister, so he was now carrying her on his back. It gave him more peace of mind to have the child's chest against him so he could feel her breathing and the beating of her heart. His legs trembled after walking uphill for so long, not to mention from the extra weight. Kevin managed to keep going thanks to fear and sheer willpower. He let out a grunt as he wondered how much battery his flashlight had left, growing more worried with each step.

A growl just behind his ear completely paralyzed him. Kevin didn't dare to move a muscle as putrid breath warmed his neck. He frowned in a mixture of disgust and terror, and caught a glimpse of movement out of the corner of his eye. The seven-foot-tall monster hunched over next to him until its shark-like fangs were at Kevin's eye level. It was as if the beast were taking a close look at him. A predator playing with its prey, it savored its dominance over him before eating him alive.

He wanted to scream, to demand the creature to stop the games and end it once and for all. However, out of his mouth came only a barely audible whine. He had come so far, and to lose it all just like that.

Leave her.

No, he couldn't leave her. How could he even think something like that? Except it wasn't a mere thought. It was an impulse, and an alien one at that. It was as if somebody else had grabbed him with strings like a puppet's and commanded him to let her go. He resisted the urge.

A sharp, indescribable pain pierced his head, and Kevin fell to his knees as his vision blurred. A burning sensation started running through his body. He recognized it instantly. It was the same feeling he had when Rob spit that black shit in his face. Kevin lowered his gaze and looked at his arms. Through the tears in his sweater, he could see black veins popping out of his biceps.

What the hell is happening to me? This time it was his own thoughts. *I'm infected with that shit. And if that's the case, is Jenny infected too?*

The deformed face of the beast was now right in front of him. His eyes darted up, desperately seeking to avoid that black gaze, but the cure was worse than the disease. Above him, two more creatures were crawling along the ceiling, their sharp claws piercing the stone. They both let go of their grip and fell beside him with a clatter. Kevin's whole body trembled frantically.

Leave her.

Again, those damn voices whispering inside his head. He felt his fingers weaken, their grip loosening on his sister's thigh.

"No!" he yelled at the top of his lungs. "Get out of my head!"

The creatures around him stood vigilant. The voices didn't seem to come from them. Nothing made any sense. Kevin put a foot to the ground and pushed himself back up again. He felt a huge weight fall on his shoulders as if Jenny was getting heavier by the second. It was them, he was sure of it. He was now turning into one of those atrocities and becoming part of some sort of fucked up hive mind. They were trying to control him.

"N-No…" Kevin managed to mumble, moving his head from side to side.

Leave her, the voices insisted, *you are safe here*.

"How do I know you fucking puppets aren't going to tear me up the moment I give her to you?" Kevin yelled, daring to be bold since he had nothing more to lose. It was all or nothing, but the truth was that he had never been more afraid in his life.

"They only do what they are ordered," said a voice, a real one, behind him.

Kevin turned over his shoulder. It was the masked man in black. His face was covered by a blank mask with only two huge black eyes, the leather wrapping around his skull and seemingly attached to his face. He wore a long black coat that reached his knees. It was him: the stalker; the one responsible for all of his suffering.

"T-tell them to go away," Kevin mumbled.

The masked man gestured into the air. The beasts shrieked in unison, one of them roaring at Kevin and letting out spurts of putrid saliva mere inches from his face. The creatures got on all fours and scurried into the darkness. Kevin stared in disbelief at the man, if that could be called a man.

Kevin's shuddering lips uttered a question: "Are you the Devil?"

"I have many names," said the man. His voice was deep and somehow alien. It sounded distant but close at the same time. "They are all the same anyway."

"W-why?" Kevin asked with a lump in his throat. "Why her? Why us?"

"Come, and I'll show you."

"No," said Kevin shaking his head and ready to go straight to the exit. But his legs wouldn't respond. He thought it was fear at first, yet as he tried to run, he realized he physically could not move them.

His head began to spin and his vision blurred until he could barely see what was in front of him. The man in the mask was trying to control him, and he had to resist it. He had to do it for Jenny. Somehow, he knew that Jenny wasn't infected. He could feel it. There was something in those creatures. He felt some sort of familiarity to them, but with

Jenny, he didn't feel anything. He knew it was because he was infected and she wasn't. How she had managed to stay clear after so long was a mystery, but he wasn't going to let it all go to shit, especially not when he was so close to saving her.

"You are not gonna do anything," said Kevin. The words crawled out of his mouth with difficulty. "You can't do anything to me, not as long as I have her. That's why your puppets didn't touch me, isn't it? What makes her so important that they don't even dare touch me?"

"The younger they are, the harder it is to convert them," said the man in black. "It takes days, even weeks for children to be integrated. If we try to force the process on them, they die."

Just like Rudy, he thought.

"Exactly," the man said.

Nothing made any sense, everything around him seemed to be part of a very long, torturous nightmare. He could feel his mind slowly fading, like somebody who's aware they're falling asleep but can't help it. Even so, he was able to connect the pieces of the puzzle, and the horrible realization that his suspicions were true hit him.

"So I was right. Those things, those monsters. They were human."

"In a past life."

His stomach turned, ready to puke what little it had left. Nausea took over, and the cave started to spin around him. That thing, whatever it was, was now inside him. It was becoming part of him, or rather, he was becoming part of It.

"What are you? What the fuck are you?"

"My first memories are blurred and unfinished."

Suddenly, his head began to ache as if his skull had been struck with an ax. Several images started to leap into his mind, some vivid and some cloudy. He could feel multiple people. He could see what they saw and feel what they felt. He had absolute power over them. That, however, was only for a fraction of a second in which he didn't even know who he was. For a fleeting moment, Kevin ceased to exist.

He struggled to get that out of his mind as he tried to get a hold on reality. He could almost feel his mind wrapped in an abyss of darkness, where he knew he would be trapped forever if he didn't fight back. He remembered Sofia, his father, and Jenny. The entity was trying to force its way into his mind, mingling with his memories. He could clearly see what the landscape looked like when they arrived, how beautiful the sunset was over the mountains, his sister's laughter while they played in the park, and Sofia's tear sliding down her cheek as he held her in the woods.

"Get out of my head!" Kevin screamed, slamming his head into the cold wall of the cave without realizing it.

Keep yourself grounded in reality, he told himself. *You can't go crazy, not now.*

That man, that entity, its existence made no sense at all. Was it a demon who took possession of its victims to unleash chaos? Some parasitic alien who found a new home in human bodies? He remembered what Wolf had told him, that the tribes used to believe disembodied spirits used living beings as hosts. Was the masked man in black one of them?

The pain in his temple increased, like drilling inside of his skull. Kevin screamed.

The man's back began to swell, creating a hump that grew until the coat he wore was torn in half. Black tentacles emerged. His suit fell to the ground, revealing a naked torso full of throbbing veins and pulsating red tissue. His whole body looked like an exposed organ. The man raised his hand, his fingers had been replaced by claws and took off his mask. His face was disfigured. Half of it was black and grimy. He had three extra eyes on his forehead for a total of five. His human side seemed severely wounded as if he had been under the tire of a speeding car.

Kevin's knees shivered, ready to drop to the ground, but he resisted the temptation to surrender. It would have been very easy to let go, give his sister to that monstrous thing and accept their fate, but that was the coward's way out. His mind screamed what he had once said before: *If there's even a remote possibility that I can save my sister, I'll take it no matter what.*

Still holding his sister tightly, he slipped his hand inside his jacket.

"I have a flare gun." Huge drops of sweat slid down his face. "If you move even an inch, I'll shoot and blow us all to bits."

The monster rose. It seemed to grow taller with each breath. Kevin drew his pistol and aimed it at the beast.

"Don't do it!" yelled a familiar voice behind him.

Kevin stopped, his finger resting unsteadily on the trigger. Norman James stood behind him, his legs planted on the floor and his arms up in the air. He looked ready to leap at the monster at any moment.

The beast's tentacles were moving frantically, producing a bubbling sound that would make anyone gag. Kevin stepped back until he was shoulder to shoulder with the agent. The monster showed its deformed fangs. Among them appeared a long, swirling tongue with a sharp end that looked made out of metal.

"Take her," Kevin whispered.

"What?" James shouted. "Are you fucking crazy? They'll kill you!"

"Let them try."

Kevin sank to his knees, turning his back on James. The agent hesitated for a second, but finally went through with it. James grabbed the girl under her armpits and pulled her into his arms. Kevin gripped the pistol firmly with both hands, pointing it straight at the monster. He glanced at the agent, who was still in place, stiff as a statue.

"Come on, Kevin."

"Leave and take her as far as possible. They won't attack you while you're holding her."

"I'm not leaving you here."

"They won't attack me if I have the power to blow them up."

The creature roared in response. Kevin's headache was getting worse by the second. He didn't know how much time he had left before it took over his mind.

"Go," Kevin begged. "Please, keep her safe."

James tried to protest; however, what came out of his mouth was, "I'll come back for you."

He took one last look at the tentacle monster before running away.

"Tell your pets not to follow them," Kevin demanded.

We'll find her sooner or later.

He knew that the monsters speaking in his mind were telling the truth. No matter where they went, they would always live in fear. He couldn't accept that. He wanted Jenny to grow up in a safe world, with the freedom to be happy without having to look over her shoulder. He had to put an end to this once and for all.

The creature rose threateningly, the slimy tentacles on its back rubbing each other. It opened its mouth to expose its fangs and sharp tongue, mere inches from Kevin's face. Seeing that thing from close up repulsed him immeasurably.

Lower the weapon, the creature commanded.

For a split second, Kevin's arms obeyed. They went down just a few inches before he regained control over them. He could maintain control for a little while longer. His head, his whole body really, ached in pain, but he would not budge until his sister was safe. There was no way out, he knew that, but he was going to take all of those demons out with him.

Overwhelming darkness began to take hold of him. He was losing the battle. It was now or never. Kevin closed his eyes and accepted his fate.

I'm okay with this. Be good, Jenny. I'll meet Mom and Dad, and we'll take care of you. I love you.

Those were Kevin Miller's last thoughts before he pulled the trigger.

CHAPTER 37

~

Soaked with sweat and blood, Norman James ran as fast as his legs allowed him. His thighs burned with every step. His shoulder prickled so much that the pain had spread to half of his torso. Jenny slept peacefully on his back, unaware of the danger she was in. His panting echoed through the tunnel, at the end of which he could see a cloudy sky inviting him to freedom.

The cold night air welcomed him as soon as he set foot on the rocky terrain. A stiff breeze hit him, carrying the snow with it, and he felt as if ice had touched his bones. He zigzagged his way through the pines right outside the coal mine and saw a squad car parked, or instead crashed, on the side. Whoever drove it that far had to be insane. He saw the driver exit the vehicle and sprint at a supernatural speed toward the mines. It was Cleyton, what was left of him at least. The mutations on his body and face made him barely recognizable, but James knew it was him.

James stopped and crouched in the bushes as he saw the lieutenant run into the tunnel. He hadn't seen them.

Good, now let's get the fuck outta here.

The agent ran through the forest, guided only by the sound of running water. Once he had found the river, he would know where to go. However, after running for what felt like miles, an invisible force propelled him forward, causing him to fall face-first into the rocks. A wave of heat embraced him, and a deafening roar flooded the forest. The branches of the trees jumped and flew in all directions.

His face hit the mud and snow. Now his whole body screamed in pain, telling him not to fight and to faint right there. He ignored the plea. He put one knee against the ground to push himself up. His hands remained firmly on Jenny's thighs, holding her against his back. Fortunately, he had received the worst of the blow.

Beside him, a pine fell on top of another. James turned and witnessed the blaze coming out of the tunnel. A wave of fire swallowed the trees around it. It danced and spread in a matter of seconds, illuminating the night in a yellow glow.

"Kevin," he whispered.

The mine spat flames incessantly. Everything inside had been instantly disintegrated. With red, watery eyes, filled with anger and awe, James continued his way back to the town to find somewhere to hide with Jenny until dawn. It was his best option; with such an explosion the whole forest would be reduced to ashes in a matter of a few hours.

Over the next couple of days, the news would call it the worst wildfire in the state's history. The blast would leave an eternal blaze in the bowels of the mines, forcing the remaining survivors of the town to leave everything behind.

CHAPTER 38

Golden beams of sunlight peeked through the tree branches. The cemetery was now almost entirely empty and devoid of life. In front of them stood a memorial to the victims of Heaven's Peak, a statue of an eagle flapping its wings, ready to take flight. At the base of the statue was a plaque with the names of hundreds of people. Among the names were Kevin and John Miller, right next to the Everett family.

James felt a hand tighten in his. Jenny was sobbing silently. Sofia and Lia had been hugging for some time, refusing to let go of each other. The four of them were the last ones remaining. The ceremony had ended almost two hours ago, and everyone else who had attended was gone.

It had been a year since those horrific events, but he remembered them every night. Jenny did too. She now slept in the same room as him, as it was the only way she wouldn't have night terrors. James adopted her a few weeks after what the media called the Great Fire of

Heaven's Peak when he discovered that there was no guardian fit for the girl. The state would have sent her to an adoption center.

He had been with her when she woke up the morning after the events.

The morning sun had revealed a desolate, completely burned-out, barren land. Several squad cars, fire trucks, and ambulances from the neighboring town had arrived. The helicopters had appeared soon after. The news had said that an explosion took place inside the mines due to natural gases, which caused the wildfire and reached the town. The testimonies of the few survivors who told the authorities what had happened were ignored. Their stories were labeled as "a case of collective hysteria." At first, it had been a highly discussed topic. Dozens of people claimed to have seen demons in the streets as well as family and friends killing each other. Then the conversations had disappeared, swept under the rug as if nothing had happened. Hundreds of people had died, and thousands had been forced to leave their homes. Yet, the world continued to spin, indolent and indifferent.

Sofia let go of her sister. Both had red faces and puffy eyes. They exchanged sweet words that James could not hear. Lia smiled and wrapped her arms around Sofia again. They would be fine. They would take care of each other, finish their studies and have successful careers. The agent had already recommended them of several universities where they could have scholarships. They had applied and, because of the situation they were in, it was only a matter of time before one of the universities responded with a letter of acceptance. He was sure the girls could take care of themselves.

He, for his part, was afraid. Although he had been involved in cases with horrific criminals and witnessed bizarre events, he had never been a father. He didn't know anything about raising a child. Jenny turned to look at him immediately as if she knew what he was thinking. She smiled weakly with her bright eyes like she was trying to say, *Don't worry, we'll be just fine.*

He would file his resignation with the FBI and start a new life. Maybe he would come back in a few years, once Jenny was older, but he couldn't make any promises. All he knew for sure was that he would try his best to raise the little girl and give her the life she deserved.

Would you like to leave a review?

As an author, I highly appreciate the feedback I get from my readers. Reviews also help others to make an informed decision before buying. If you enjoyed this book, please consider leaving a short review.

Made in the USA
Monee, IL
06 June 2022

97603886R00173